Road to Danger

Road to Danger

The date from hell...

Mallory Cook is on the worst blind date of her life. She and Carter Anderson have little in common and she can't wait for the night to end. Sure, he's gorgeous and sexy but clearly he knows it. A man with this much self-esteem isn't someone she wants in her life. She might have been desperate enough to get fixed up with him once but she's not desperate enough to do it twice. She'd rather spend the evening with Netflix.

Can't end soon enough...

Carter has been out with many women in his lifetime but this one takes the cake. They have nothing to talk about and she hasn't laughed at any of his jokes. It's amazing how incredibly long one night can feel. He can't wait to drop her off and then head straight to his favorite watering hole.

But neither one of them is going to get their wish. When Carter pulls over at a rest stop to change a tire, Mallory heads to the ladies' room to freshen up. That's when the date really goes down hill.

Because a mysterious bleeding man has just died in her arms...

Road to Danger

Danger Incorporated

Book Eight

BY

OLIVIA JAYMES

www.OliviaJaymes.com

Chapter One

THIS WASN'T THE worst date Mallory Cook had ever been on. There had been that one where her date's wife had shown up at the restaurant halfway through dinner. That had been awkward, especially as she hadn't known her date was married. It appeared he didn't know as well because Mallory had the distinct feeling that this wasn't the first time the wife had busted up an illicit evening.

There had also been the time she'd been asked to go to a baseball game and she'd assumed it was to watch but then when they arrived she'd found out it was to play. Mallory was not athletic. She'd tried to tough it out but eventually they'd pulled her from the game when they'd realized she had terrible eye-hand coordination. Apparently that was a skill that her date highly prized because he never called her again. She hadn't been upset about it.

And tonight? Tonight might not have been the worst date but it was in the top five of all time. New in the area, she'd been set up with Carter Anderson by a mutual acquaintance who kept saying that Mallory was the perfect match for him.

I don't know what she was smoking but I am not a perfect

match.

It had only been after she'd agreed to go out on the blind date that she'd heard about Carter's reputation with females in the tri-county area. He was something of a legend, dating eligible women for miles around. He didn't stay with one for long though, taking the honey bee and flower approach to relationships. He'd been described as sexy, handsome, and "over the top", whatever that meant.

In other words, while Mallory had been faithfully dating her boyfriend of six years, Carter had been sleeping around. He wasn't exactly her Prince Charming but she'd been willing to keep an open mind.

If he dates every woman I suppose it was only a matter of time before he got to me.

Mallory and Carter had had dinner, seen a movie, and were now driving toward her home in Green Pine which was about forty-five minutes from Tremont. She had long given up trying to talk to him so the trip was quiet, only the sound of the satellite radio playing softly in the background and the hum of the tires on the road. The inside of the car was warm though, despite the dropping temperatures outside.

The bad evening wasn't all his fault. She had to take some of the blame, too. If she'd been a different sort of person she might have had more patience with all of the interruptions. She might have asked him more questions, although he'd done a pretty good job of talking about himself on the rare occasions he'd spoken to her. She was funny that way. At thirty-one years of age, she expected the man to be interested in her, wanting to know more about her life. Carter hadn't acted that way at all. It was like he'd taken her out because he'd lost a bet.

Which wasn't out of the realm of possibility.

All Mallory wanted to do was end this evening with as much dignity as possible. Be friendly. Thank him for dinner and the movie. Smile and be genuine. He had insisted on picking up the check, although she had made more than one offer to do so. That alone deserved a thank you. She'd act as if she'd had a good time and then go inside her house, closing the door behind her. She wasn't concerned about turning him down for a second date because she was sure he wouldn't ask. In fact, she was positive he wasn't even going to go in for a goodnight kiss. There simply hadn't been any chemistry between them. Too bad, because Carter Anderson was a looker.

Dark hair clipped short. Light blue eyes. Wide shoulders and a strong jaw. He was yummy and it was no surprise why he did so well with the ladies. He even had a dimple in his cheek when he smiled.

They were still about twenty minutes from Green Pine and freedom when she heard him curse under his breath.

"Shit, the tire pressure light just came on. I need to check the tires. One might be going flat."

Changing the tire on the side of a dimly lit highway didn't sound all that safe. He had slowed down considerably but hadn't pulled over yet.

"I saw a sign for a rest stop up a few miles. It would be better lit than the side of the road."

To her surprise, he turned and smiled at her. "That's a great idea. I'd forgotten all about it. Sorry about this but I really do need to check."

Safety first and all of that. It wouldn't do to get stranded with him in the middle of the night. That would only prolong this torture.

"It's fine. Do whatever you need to do."

Carter kept the vehicle at a reasonable speed for the next mile and a half, exiting at the rest stop and pulling up near the door of the building. As she'd predicted, it was better lit, especially where they'd parked. There were other cars there as well, including a family in a minivan which made Mallory feel much safer. The thought of a deserted rest stop in the middle of the night was kind of creepy. Clearly she'd watched too many horror movies. Luckily a man in a hockey mask wouldn't be an issue. A car had even pulled in right after them, joining the vehicles already there.

Since Carter got out of the car Mallory did too, wanting to help by checking the tires on her side of the vehicle. She wouldn't mind stretching her legs either. It didn't feel right to simply sit and wait when she could be of some help. She'd learned to change a tire when she was a teen. Her father had insisted on it. If for some reason Carter didn't know how, she could be of some use.

The cold wind hit her like a brick wall and she shivered in her too thin coat. She should have checked the weather before dressing this evening but she'd been more worried about looking nice than being warm. Even if she had known about the temperature, she wouldn't have expected to be standing outside for any length of time this evening.

"These look okay," she said, peering around the back of the car to where Carter had disappeared. He was kneeling next to the driver's side back tire with a grim expression. The tire looked a little flat but not horrible. It would need to be changed, though. "You found it."

He nodded, rubbing his chin. "I did. We might have picked up a nail somewhere."

There had been some construction going on across the street from the movie theatre.

"Do you have a spare?"

Levering up, he came to the back of the car where she was standing and she caught a whiff of his aftershave or body wash. He smelled pretty good for a bad date. "I do but it's just one of those stupid donuts. I guess it's better than nothing. I'll get this changed and we can get back on the road. I'm sorry about this."

"It's not your fault. Can I help?"

It must have been the last thing he'd expected her to say because he blinked a few times before answering. "Thank you but no, I've got this. You can go wait in the car if you like. The temperature has dropped quite a bit. You're probably cold."

"You have to be cold, too." She pointed to his bare forearms where he'd rolled up his shirt sleeves in preparation for changing the tire. He wasn't even wearing a jacket. Men were so stupid sometimes, acting all macho. He was probably freezing his boys off but didn't want to admit it. "How about I see if there's a hot coffee machine in there?"

"Actually, I could go for a soda, if you don't mind? The cold really doesn't bother me. My brothers and cousins would throw me out in the snow just for fun and then lock the door."

He didn't seem like a guy that would allow that to happen. She wouldn't have let her older siblings toss her out into the snow. That was crazy.

She couldn't stop herself from asking. "And you just let them?"

Chuckling, he smiled and it looked rather evil. "They were bigger than me and there were more of them. I was the youngest so I had to be smarter. I always got them back, trust me on this."

This was the best conversation they'd had all evening. His phone hadn't rung once on the drive home.

"Thanksgiving at your house must have been a riot."

"It still is. We may be grown up but get us all in a room together and we act like little kids. Last year our mom threatened to put us in time out. And my oldest brother is over forty."

It actually sounded fun. And heartwarming. And kind of sweet.

"Just so we're clear I only know some basic first aid. If you get frostbite you're on your own. One soda coming up. Diet or regular?"

He shoved his hand into his pocket and pulled out several one-dollar bills and a five. To his credit he wasn't a cheapskate.

"Regular. And get yourself whatever you'd like, too."

"Thanks."

Mallory headed into the brick building and immediately found the vending machines along the far wall. A woman was standing in front of the soda machine with a bottle of water in her hand.

"I'll be done in a sec," the woman said with a friendly smile. "My husband needs the caffeine to stay awake."

She must be with the minivan.

A can of Coke dispensed with a thunk and the woman fished

it out of the machine's well before nodding and walking toward the entrance. Quickly Mallory fed two dollar bills into the machine and pushed the button. The can loudly fell and she fed it more money, but this time getting one without caffeine for herself. Otherwise she'd be up all night.

Wrapping her jacket more tightly around her, she headed back out into the cold where Carter had the tire off and was putting the donut into place. Despite assuring her that the weather didn't bother him, she still felt badly that he was having to change the tire. "Here you go," she said, placing the can on the ground next to him. "I think I'm going to run to the ladies' room."

Carter grunted as he reached for the hubcap with the lug nuts rolling around inside. "Take your time. I'll need to make a pit stop before we go, too."

She turned but stopped, instead asking him a question before she left him to finish.

"Were those air or hand tightened?"

If they were the former, he'd have had a bitch of a time getting them off, and there was no way she would have been able to do it.

The question made him grin, showing off that dimple again. "Air and I won't make that mistake again."

He'd been…surprisingly pleasant to deal with since they'd pulled into the rest stop. If he'd acted like this all evening things might have turned out much differently. There might have been a second date.

Alas, it simply wasn't to be.

Chapter Two

CARTER SHOVED THE flat tire into the trunk and slammed it shut. Wiping his hands on a towel he'd found in his gym bag, he checked his phone for another message. One of his buddies was at the hospital tonight with his wife. She was in labor and his friend had been texting him all evening long keeping Carter and everyone else in the loop. Normally that would have been fine but it had played havoc with his date.

Mallory didn't seem to appreciate the constant interruptions and he really should explain, although he wasn't sure that this date was going anywhere. The evening had been mediocre at best and he'd been glad when it was time to drive her home. She was an extremely attractive woman with her dark hair, golden-brown eyes, and curvy figure. He was a boob man through and through and Mallory Cook was perfection in that department. Not too big and not too small. Like in the Three Bears his mother used to read to him when he was little, Mallory was just right.

She might be his physical match but personality-wise she just wasn't his type. Every time he'd tried to engage her in conversation she'd stayed stubbornly silent. At first he'd thought that perhaps she was shy, but eventually he'd come to the conclusion that she didn't want to talk to him.

When he'd agreed to this date he'd heard quite a bit about her. She had dated someone for a long time but they'd broken up about a year ago. That's when she'd moved to Green Pine to teach math. His friend had said that Mallory was pretty, funny, intelligent, and kind. He couldn't argue with any of that – except maybe the funny part. She hadn't laughed at any of his jokes tonight and that hit a man hard in the ego. But she was smart and kind. She'd remembered the rest stop and she'd offered to get him a coffee which was nice. Maybe a second date wasn't out of the question after all.

Except he didn't think she was all that attracted to him. Carter prided himself on knowing women and when they were into him. And Mallory? She didn't seem to care if he lived or died. Not in a cruel way but more in a "she'd be fine if she never saw him again" kind of way. Another ego buster.

Carter and Mallory needed to get going as well but first he wanted to make a quick trip to the restroom. He headed into the building, pausing to hold the door for the lady from another vehicle. She gave him a small smile.

"Thank you."

"You're welcome, ma'am."

His mama had raised him right. Open doors. Pull out chairs. Say please and thank you. Don't put your elbows on the table and don't eat like a hog at a trough.

Once inside, Mallory was nowhere in sight. She must still be in the ladies' room. There was something about her. He didn't know what it was but he hadn't really given her much of a chance tonight. He'd been dragged kicking and screaming into this date but she was what had been promised. He hadn't exactly been the perfect escort either. Distracted by his friend, Carter could have tried harder to engage her in conversation. Get to know her a little. What had he even asked her? He didn't remember since he'd been so distracted.

They didn't have much of a drive home left but Carter was going to try and be nice to her the rest of the way. Try and make her laugh. Salvage what he could of the evening. They might even go out on another date.

✦   ✦   ✦

MALLORY SMOOTHED DOWN her windblown hair and then applied a fresh coat of lipstick. This was about as presentable as she was going to get. She made a face at herself in the mirror and then slipped the lipstick tube back into her purse. The date was almost at an end. Carter would drive her home and then she'd never have to see him again.

He'd been nice since the flat tire, though. Smiling and friendly in a way that he hadn't been before. His phone had been blessedly silent the last few minutes and she wondered if perhaps he had something going on at work to be getting all of those messages. Or perhaps he was just rude. She didn't know because he hadn't said a word about them, simply tapping away at his phone and ignoring her.

If only he'd been this guy all night. It would have been a heck of a lot more enjoyable.

Pushing open the door of the ladies' room she headed out of the warm, well-lit building and out into the cold night air. The bite of the wind immediately undid any work she'd done on her hair, and she wrapped her coat a little more tightly around her. The temperature was definitely dropping and since it was only around midnight it still had further to go.

She stopped on the sidewalk in front of the building, realizing Carter wasn't in or around the car. He must have gone inside for that pit stop and that meant she was alone. Not that there was anyone to be worried about. The rest area had cleared out while she was in the restroom but it was well-lit and quiet. The only two vehicles that were left were the sedan to their right and Mallory and Carter. The driver couldn't be far away because he'd left the driver's side door open.

Hopefully her date had left her door unlocked so she could wait in the much warmer car. She headed for the passenger side and reached for the handle but her hand fell away and her stomach roiled in her abdomen. Rushing to the back of the car next to them and almost tripping over her own feet, she found a man in a pool of what appeared to be his own blood. A trickle of the red liquid dripped from the corner of his mouth and he reached up to grab her arms, his grip surprisingly strong. There was a metallic smell to the air and bile rose in her throat, making any words she might have tried to speak impossible.

"Help m–"

Kneeling next to him, Mallory fought down the nausea and panic. Her heart was racing and the blood roared in her ears, blocking out the rest of the world. She had to keep her wits about her and think straight. She sucked in a crisis and this was a big one. Should she try CPR or mouth to mouth? He was struggling to breathe but there was a large wet stain on the front of his shirt that made her think chest compressions were a bad idea. Her own clothes were becoming red and sodden as well as his fingers dug into the fabric of her jacket.

With one hand, she tried to pull her phone from her purse but her entire body was shaking, making it ten times harder than it should have been. "I'll call for help. I'll call 911. Just hold on, okay? Okay?"

Her voice came out as a squeak but the man didn't answer. He made a few guttural and none too healthy-sounding noises as she fumbled with her phone, desperately trying to hurry while remembering her passcode at the same time. A gasp came from his lips and then he was quiet. Strangely his grip didn't loosen but his pale skin and still chest told her that he was gone. She was going to call 911 regardless but they probably didn't need to hurry.

A man had just died in her arms.

Chapter Three

RED AND BLUE flashing lights illuminated the parking lot of the rest stop, alerting anyone driving by that they could speed without worrying about being pulled over.

Because every cop within a hundred-mile radius had to be at the rest stop.

Carter counted at least half a dozen cop cars, a forensic van, and two rescue units. He and Mallory had told their stories to no less than three different officers of varying rank. Frankly, he didn't have much to tell them. He hadn't seen it happen or knew who did it but surely they had cameras at these rest stops?

A sympathetic ambulance driver had wrapped Mallory up in a blanket and taken her inside the building where it was warmer. She appeared slightly dazed as if in shock and he wouldn't have blamed her if she had been. A man had died in her arms and that was going to absolutely change a person. When Carter had come out of the building and found her sitting on the ground, her clothes covered in blood and a man lying prone on the pavement, for a moment he'd thought...well...that she'd done something...terrible. He didn't know her well, after all.

It had taken some doing through her tears and sobs to get

the whole story. She'd already called 911 so he gently pulled her away from the body, moving her so she was leaning against his car. He'd checked the man's pulse and breathing before starting CPR but blood simply gushed out of the wounds in his chest. Carter had tried mouth to mouth but the victim was unresponsive. By the time the ambulance and cops arrived, he was sure there wasn't anything that they could do.

Sliding closer to Mallory on the bench, he tentatively placed his arm around her shoulders. She looked so fragile and scared like she could break at any moment. Visibly trembling, she didn't shake off the gesture of comfort but she didn't respond either. She was somewhere far away, perhaps still sitting next to that poor man on the ground.

"Honey, can I get you anything? Something to drink? How about some water?"

For a minute he thought she hadn't heard him but then she turned to answer, her cheeks wet with tears. "I'm alright."

She sounded like Kermit the Frog so obviously she wasn't fine. The good news though was that she'd answered him. She was back in the present and that was progress.

"It's okay to be upset. It's completely normal."

Why did he say that? It sounded so fucking lame. She could do or act any way she wanted to. She didn't need his permission.

I suck at comforting people.

"He was so pale."

The words came out as barely a whisper and Carter had to bend his head to be able to hear her.

"He'd lost a lot of blood, honey."

At least that's what Carter assumed. He was no doctor, although he'd seen some nasty accidents on the construction sites he managed.

"He asked me to help him." She shook her head, her hair falling over her tearstained face. "No, he tried to ask me but he couldn't get the words out. He just made this horrible sound and then went still."

Having already heard this part of her story, Carter's own chest tightened in sympathy. This shouldn't have happened to her. If he hadn't gone inside to take a leak she wouldn't have been out there alone.

"It's my fault," he said bluntly. "If I hadn't gone inside this wouldn't have happened. A few seconds earlier and you could have been killed."

She looked up at him, shaking her head. "If you had been outside, you'd probably be dead, too."

That had occurred to him but he liked to think that he could hold his own with an assailant. Between him and the other guy, they could have taken the attacker.

Whoever "he" might be.

"I'm just glad you weren't there. I'm so fucking sorry this happened to you."

She tried to smile through the tears. "I think that poor man is having a much worse night."

There it was. She was now officially everything that had been promised. She was funny too, and at a moment that definitely needed lightening. If she could laugh while she cried she was a strong woman. At least that's what his mother always said.

Another uniformed officer approached them wearing a grim expression. His name tag said *Sergeant C. Roy.*

"Hello, I'm Sergeant Charles Roy. You two were here when Mr. Montgomery was stabbed and killed? Can you tell us what happened?"

Carter wasn't in the best of moods. They wouldn't let Mallory and himself leave even though they'd already given a statement. He was beginning to wonder if they were suspects. Should he call an attorney?

"We've already told what we know and saw," Carter replied, trying to keep his voice even and friendly but pointing out the officers they'd spoken to. "To him. Him. Her. Oh, and him, too. Did they not write it down?"

The sergeant had the decency to look uncomfortable. "I'm sure they did but I'm hoping to hear the story straight from you. If you don't mind?"

"Then can we go home?" Mallory asked softly, her voice thick with tears. She'd been put through the wringer and this guy wanted her to relive it one more time for the entertainment of the cheap seats.

The officer looked over his shoulder briefly. "I hope so. Now, Miss Cook, would you mind stepping over here with me?"

Her fingers tightened on Carter's arm and he pulled her a little closer, hopefully reassuring her that he wasn't going anywhere willingly. His cousin was a former detective so he knew what they were trying to do. Honestly, they should have done it long before now. It was standard procedure to separate them and get their stories so that the cops could compare them. They'd already fucked that up so too bad. "Miss Cook is a little unsteady right now. I'm sure you understand. She's had something of a shock tonight."

"I really need to speak with–"

"We've already told our stories in front of each other," Carter interrupted. "It's too late to separate us."

Now the officer looked not only uncomfortable but embarrassed. He checked his notebook for a moment before speaking. "Mr. Anderson, I'm now in charge of this– Wait, are you one of *those* Andersons?"

Carter had been waiting for it and was only surprised the question hadn't come before now. It was the story of his life. People treated him one way and then figured out who he was – through no help from him – and then he was treated a completely different way. Usually much better. Money talked, after all, and the Anderson family had stockpiled some serious cash and assets in the last two generations. He hated this part but there was no ducking his heritage. He'd learned to be proud and unapologetic about being an Anderson.

"I am. Is that important to this discussion?"

It was, and they both knew it, but Carter wasn't going to give this guy any help.

"Wait here."

The sergeant quickly turned on his heel and walked away, leaving Carter and Mallory alone again. A much preferred state, although he'd rather be home. If they were going to sit here in this fluorescent light hell then at least he had good company.

"What was he talking about?" Mallory's brows pinched together and she pulled away slightly. "Those Andersons? Are you part of a crime family or something?"

The way people reacted Carter sometimes felt like it. The majority didn't care one way or the other but there were a couple of other camps they could fall into. One was of the opinion that the Andersons must be doing something unethical or illegal to have made so much money. The second was that they should be feared or revered.

Where would this woman fall?

"My family owns a ranch and several businesses in the Tremont area. I run the construction arm of Anderson Industries. In addition, my cousin Jason was a DEA agent and my other cousin West was the head of detectives and is now mayor."

She glanced at the cop who was in deep conversation with another law enforcement officer and then back at Carter.

"So I'm kind of not sure why all of that matters. Does he know your cousins?"

"He might know West." Shit, he needed to just lay it on the line. "The Andersons…give to many causes and also to local, state, and national politicians that we support. The officer may feel that it's better to tread lightly in this situation."

Finally she nodded as if she understood. "You know people in high places. Is that what you're trying not to say?"

"Pretty much," he admitted. "Sometimes people treat me differently because of my last name."

"What do you think he's talking about over there? Is he going to let us leave?"

"Maybe," Carter said, although he was doubtful. They wouldn't be going anywhere until the police confirmed that they didn't have anything to do with the murder, and there was only one way to do that. The security cameras located inside and around the property. "I sent my cousin a text to ask for advice and he said to sit tight and cooperate. I guess that's what we'll do. But if you need anything, just let me know and I'll make sure you get it."

"I'd like to go to the ladies' room and wash up. Do you think they'd let me?"

The forensics team had already examined both of them head to toe and taken their clothes as evidence, giving them each a pair of sweats and sweatshirt to wear. There wasn't any reason she couldn't wash the blood off of her skin. He wouldn't mind doing that too.

Carter started to try to hail the sergeant but then stopped when he saw a familiar face striding through the doors of the building. The family attorney Bryce Franklin. West must have called him. Sagging with relief, he gave Bryce a wave.

"I don't think I've ever been so happy to see a lawyer before. Did West call you?"

"He did. This is a nasty situation. Have they taken your statements yet?"

Sighing heavily, Carter pointed to the sergeant. "Several times. They've taken our clothes and they've taken our statements, but he wants to do it again. Separate this time. I don't want Mallory to be on her own. She's been through more than enough tonight."

Bryce turned his attention to Mallory, giving her an encouraging smile. "You've had a difficult night so let me see what I can do to get you out of here, okay? I'm Bryce Franklin, by the way."

He held out his hand and Mallory started to extend hers, then pulled it back with a wince as she realized she still had blood on her skin. "Mallory Cook. And thank you."

"Just hang in there. I've got this."

Carter hoped to hell he did. They hadn't killed that man but there was someone out there who had. That's who the cops needed to be focusing on, not two innocent people on a mediocre date.

Chapter Four

CARTER UNLOCKED THE front door of Mallory's little townhouse in Green Pine and ushered her inside. She'd tried to do it herself but her hands were still shaking from her experience at the rest stop. He'd offered to call someone to stay with her but she didn't want to wake any of her friends in the middle of the night. Her parents had semi-retired and spent the winters in Florida so they couldn't be of any comfort tonight. At least until morning, she was on her own.

He didn't like that one bit. He'd been raised to be a gentleman and it didn't feel very chivalrous to leave her here all by herself when she was so shaken up. Only someone mean and uncaring would dump her here and wave as they drove away.

"I can stay," Carter offered again for the sixth or seventh time. She'd steadfastly refused, although he could feel her weakening with every denial that she needed help. The closer he came to leaving, the more real it was becoming to her. "It's no big deal. I could just sack out on the couch."

It looked overstuffed and comfy with its striped cushions and multitude of throw pillows. On any other occasion, he could definitely catch a few zzz's there. Tonight? That was a hell of a lot more iffy. As for Mallory, she didn't look like she ever wanted to close her eyes again.

"I'm fine," she replied, trying to appear stoic but the words came out tremulous and thready. "I'll be okay. Maybe I'll just watch television or something until the sun comes up."

I'd be an asshole to leave her. Maybe I could just sleep in the car outside.

"That sounds like a terrible plan. Being frightened for hours isn't a good option."

The corners of her mouth turned up slightly. "It's four in the morning. The sun will be up in a couple of hours."

This time of year it would be more like three and a half but the details didn't matter much. The truth was he didn't want to leave her and she didn't want him to go. She was just being stubborn. There was no guarantee that the light of day would make her feel any better.

Carter opened his mouth to reply but didn't get the chance. A metallic whooshing sound had her crying out in fear and she whirled around, her entire body tensed as if for fight or flight. He wasn't sure which and they didn't need to find out. In two seconds he'd crossed the short distance between them and wrapped his arms around her trembling body, pulling her close. Despite being stuck in a dingy rest stop most of the night she still smelled lovely, like vanilla and something softly floral. It might just have been her shampoo but he was like many men and adored that women smelled so much better than their male counterparts.

"Easy there, honey. It's just your refrigerator. Probably the ice maker, to be exact. Mine makes the same noise."

Mallory took a few deep breaths and then eased out of his arms, putting some distance between them. "Yes, it's just the ice maker. Sorry. I guess...I am a little jumpy."

She was a whole lot more than that and she knew it.

"There's no shame in feeling out of sorts after what you've experienced tonight. Anyone would feel the same way."

Not answering right away, she rubbed her hands along her arms as if she was cold. The house wasn't freezing but the thermostat could definitely stand to be bumped up a few degrees. "I guess so."

"There's no guessing here. I've seen grown men lose their lunch at far less."

Her brows shot up and her expression turned suspicious. "For real?"

"Absolutely. One of my men on a construction site hurt himself. I won't go into the details but he was bleeding from his hand and another guy saw it and puked. He couldn't take it. So you're doing better than he is. Not once have you vomited."

"I wanted to a couple of times."

So did he.

"But you didn't. You're strong but maybe this isn't the exact moment to prove that. No one would blame you if you wanted to wrap yourself up in a blanket and drink hot chocolate with lots of marshmallows."

That's what his mother would have done for her if she'd been here.

"That sounds wonderful right now."

"I'll make you some," he offered, relieved to see that she was beginning to be honest about how shook she was. Denial wasn't going to help. "I make a mean hot chocolate."

It was an Anderson family special recipe.

"Can you make it out of yogurt and apples?"

"No, why?"

She nodded toward the kitchen. "Because that's all I have to eat. I'm a rotten cook and usually eat out. I only have the yogurt and apples for when I need a snack."

Carter couldn't imagine any woman admitting that she couldn't cook. They all seemed to want to make him dinner and show off what a good little wife they'd be. Little did they realize that fixing him a meal wasn't any part of his criteria for a lifetime mate.

"You can't cook? Really?"

Maybe it was something she simply said so that no one expected her to do it.

"I can barely boil water," she sighed. "I've tried many times but trust me when I say that nothing good has ever come out of a kitchen with me in it. So I'm afraid that I'm going to have to decline the offer of hot chocolate even though it sounded wonderful."

Carter had milk. And cocoa. He even had marshmallows, thanks to the cookout the Anderson family had had a few weekends ago.

Just like that, he made up his mind.

"Let's get you a bag packed. You're not staying here."

Her mouth dropped open and her eyes widened. "I—What do you mean?"

"You're coming home with me."

Those eyes had narrowed and she was giving him a look that

said he was full of shit. Yep, this woman was definitely growing on him. She didn't take any crap.

"We're both shook up," he explained, guiding her down what he hoped was a hall to her bedroom, his hands gently on her shoulders. "Honest to God, I don't think either one of us should be alone right now. I have an extra bedroom and a big yellow Lab that will smother you with slobbery kisses but he'd rip the leg off of an intruder. You can feel safe there, maybe even get some sleep. When you wake up, if you want to leave, I won't try and stop you."

She stopped in the middle of the hallway and turned to study him. Standing very still under her scrutiny, he took the opportunity to do the same. There was determination in her eyes but he could see the fear that lurked there as well. She was torn in two, wanting to be strong but not wanting to be alone.

"Listen, I'm a nice guy. I know that our date kind of sucked and I'm really sorry about that. That's my fault, too. But I truly just want to protect you. You'll be behind gates and a security system. Believe me, there is no safer place in Montana."

Her brow arched and she crossed her arms over her chest. "And just where is this oasis of personal safety?"

The Anderson ranch.

Chapter Five

IT SHOULDN'T HAVE felt so comfortable to be in Carter's company. They'd had a crappy date and she should have pushed him out of her front door but there was something about him that made her feel safe. Especially at this moment when she didn't feel safe in the least. Her brain knew good and well that she wasn't in any danger. No one wanted her dead or was coming after her. But her emotions? Jangled and in a spin. She didn't know up from down, right from left, or her ice maker from a serial killer.

Honestly, she simply didn't want to be alone.

Which is how she found herself sitting next to him in his car as he drove down a long road to the Anderson ranch. Considering it had been over fifteen minutes since they'd entered the front gate, this place had to be huge, which kind of made sense considering how the officer's demeanor had quickly changed when finding out that Carter was one of *those* Andersons. Whatever that meant. She could have done a quick Google search on her phone about the family but it seemed like a strange way to get to know someone. If she had questions, she simply needed to open her mouth and ask them like a grownup.

"I guess the ranch is pretty big."

Not exactly a question. More like an observation but it seemed to do the trick. Carter glanced over at her, giving her a reassuring smile. He really wasn't the jerk she'd thought several hours ago.

"It's the largest privately held ranch in Montana. I swear we're not criminals. Just a family trying to do the best they can for themselves and their community. My parents are terrific people. Mom is going to want to coddle you so you should probably just let her. It's easier than arguing, I've found. Now that she doesn't have her brood to fuss over she takes any chance she can get to go into Super Mom mode."

That sounded sweet but Mallory didn't want to be a bother. She already felt terrible that she was such a wuss she couldn't be alone.

"I hope your cousin didn't wake them."

"You can hope all you want," he chuckled. "But I'm guessing that every Anderson is out of bed right now based on the fact that the family attorney showed up at the rest stop. Mom is probably frying bacon right about now. Or maybe pancakes. Or both."

Carter nodded toward a structure that had appeared on the horizon. "And the house is lit up like an airport. Just as I sus-pected."

They were closer now and Mallory could see that indeed just about every light in the two-story home was on. There were several cars parked around it and as they pulled up a yellow Lab bounded out of the front door and down the porch steps.

Carter climbed out and was immediately circled by a tail

wagging and barking canine. He paused to pet the dog but didn't linger, coming around to her side of the vehicle, Lab on his heels.

"Tiger, this is Mallory. Mallory, this is Tiger. Pet him and he's your friend for life. You aren't afraid of dogs, are you?"

"Not at all." She bent over to receive a slobbery kiss on her cheek. Tiger was a sweetheart. She'd missed having a pet but her ex had been allergic. "I love dogs."

Tiger was also pretty well-behaved, sitting on his furry bottom when it was clear he wanted to jump up on her. The sound of footsteps captured her attention and two men were approaching them, friendly smiles on their faces. She tensed for a moment but Carter's reassuring arm around her shoulders didn't allow her to turn and run.

"That's my older brother Noah. He runs the ranch. The guy behind him is Easton, his twin. Easton runs the financial arm of Anderson Industries."

Mallory was beginning to get an inkling of what the Anderson family might represent, although she couldn't be sure. The fact that there was an *arm* for finances was a big clue though.

"And you run the construction part, right?"

When he'd told her over dinner, she'd pictured him in a yellow hardhat carrying a metal lunchpail on some dirty construction site. She had a feeling that she was way off.

"I do. We have several projects going right now including a housing development near Green Pine. It's going to have fifty luxury homes plus two hundred affordable condos."

She knew the one he was speaking about. The locals were excited because it meant jobs. She'd seen the Anderson Construction signs around the area but until this moment she hadn't put two and two together.

Noah and Easton both hugged their brother and then stepped back, waiting to be introduced.

"Mallory, this is Noah and Easton. The way to tell them apart is that Easton is always a pain in the ass and Noah...wait. You can't tell them apart that way."

The one with longer hair and a twinkle in his eye held out his hand. "Forgive my little brother. He thinks he's funny and we've humored him his whole life. I'm Noah and this uptight bastard is Easton, my younger brother by about seven minutes."

Easton didn't look uptight, although his hair was shorter and his clothes looked slightly preppy while Noah's were definitely Montana ranch.

She shook their hands. "It's nice to meet you. I've heard a little bit about you."

That you threw Carter into the snow and locked him out of the house.

"Lies, lies, lies," chanted Noah with a grin before he addressed Carter. "Mom's cooking breakfast so I hope you're hungry. Everyone's inside and they're going to want all the details."

Giving Mallory a worried glance, Carter shifted on his feet. "I brought Mallory here because she's really freaked out about what happened. I'm not sure we're ready to relive it all."

"I'm not going to be able to sleep," she found herself replying. "We might as well tell them. I've already told four cops and a reporter."

That made Carter scowl. "That asshole, sticking a camera in

your face when we were trying to leave."

"He was just doing his job."

Although he could have been nicer about it. Or more sensitive. Even the cameraman had winced when the reporter had asked her questions.

Badgered is more like it. He hadn't wanted to take *no comment* for an answer. He'd stuck that microphone in her face and when she didn't tell him everything he'd wanted to know, he'd done the same to Carter. Carter, on the other hand, wasn't as patient as she was and he'd shoved the reporter, knocking him back into the cameraman. The reporter had had the audacity to ask if they'd killed that poor man but were being let go because Carter was an Anderson.

Once again…whatever that meant.

"His job sucks," Carter said bluntly, placing his hand on her lower back and guiding her into his home. "He's a leech on society and gives good and decent reporters a bad name."

Easton growled, baring his teeth slightly. "Let me guess who it was. Dave Gorman? I bet it was him. He's had it in for the Anderson family for years."

She didn't know the answer but Carter was already nodding in the affirmative. "It was and it looks like his vendetta is still on. I have no idea what we did to piss him off."

A voice came from another room. "I put his brother in jail."

A handsome dark-haired man stepped into the living room, wiping his hands on a dishtowel. All of the Anderson men resembled each other, and they were all good-looking in their own way. Carter couldn't have been the only heartbreaker in this family.

Holy shit, the parents must look like movie stars.

He held out his hand for Mallory to shake. "I'm West, Carter's cousin. I used to be the head of detectives in Tremont."

This must be the cousin Carter had called. Thank goodness he'd sent the attorney, otherwise she had a feeling that they'd still be there telling their story over and over again.

"It's nice to meet you. Thank you so much for sending your lawyer. I was sure we'd be there all day."

Grimacing, West enfolded her hand in his much larger one. "I had a feeling that they would do that. Bryce made them pull the footage from the security cameras right away and it showed that you both had nothing to do with it. Despite the gaps in video coverage, the tape clearly showed you and then Carter exiting the building after the victim had already been wounded."

Unfortunately the actual murder and murderer hadn't also been caught on film.

"And yet they still didn't want to let us go," groused Carter. "You could tell that they wanted it to be us."

Carter and Mallory were all that the police had. Everyone else had already left when she'd come out of the restroom. Of course, the cameras showed that there were other suspects but the cops needed to find them.

The smell of eggs, bacon, and toast wafted under Mallory's nose and it actually smelled good. She was shocked that she had an appetite but the last time she'd eaten had literally been hours ago when she'd had a small popcorn at the movie.

Carter's stomach had no inhibitions and it growled loud enough to let everyone know he was hungry.

"Please tell me Mom is in the kitchen."

"What if I tell you it's Jason?" Noah teased. "He can cook, too."

"Not like Mom."

Noah slapped Carter on the back. "It's Mom and she's made a feast. I hope you both are hungry, although there might not be any food left. Jason is in there and he was filling his plate when we came out to meet you. Tiger's in there too, strategically located to get any fallout."

Carter sighed. "Mom feeds him. I think he eats more bacon than I do. Are you hungry, Mallory? Do you think you could eat a little something?"

Maybe it was the warm and friendly welcome she had received. It might have been how secure she felt with all of these people around. It could even have been the way Carter rested his hand on her back so reassuringly. Whatever it was, for the first time in hours, Mallory felt safe. One small step towards getting back to normal.

"I could eat."

Chapter Six

KATHY AND PETER Anderson, Carter's parents, were absolutely adorable. Clearly in love after all their years together, they made Mallory feel instantly at home. The food was delicious and the company even better. If this was the family that Carter had been brought up in, he couldn't be too bad of a guy.

The enormous kitchen located at the back of the house was packed to the gills with people. Normally, Mallory preferred an open floor plan but this room had its charms – the major one being the large French doors that led out onto a glassed-in patio that ran the length of the house. A dining room was off to the left with a long table that looked as if it could seat ten or twelve with ease. If she hadn't met his family this morning, she would have thought it was a strange thing for a bachelor to have in his home.

No one pushed Mallory or Carter to tell their stories. The delicious food was devoured and small talk was made. It was as if the horrible night never happened, although the tension hovered just on the periphery. It was there but for a few minutes she was able to ignore it. It wouldn't last, however. As Kathy and Noah began to gather the dirty dishes, that peace was going to come to an end.

The cousin Jason, whom she'd learned was a former DEA agent, had been quiet for most of the meal, his eyes watchful but his mouth closed. He'd been taking it all in but now that he'd finished eating he appeared to ready to speak.

"I'm glad you're okay," he said, his expression somber. "You were lucky. God knows what that poor man was involved in that got him killed but you two could have been tangled up in it and ended up hurt."

Or dead. But he didn't have to say it out loud. They were all thinking it. At least she was.

Carter nodded. "We are lucky. I just wish I'd been there for Mallory. She got the bad end of all of this."

It was silly for him to say that. He'd seen the man bloody and dying just as she had. The only thing he hadn't witnessed was the pleading for help. Mallory was sure she'd never forget that if she lived to be a hundred. She didn't even have to strain to hear the dying man's voice. She shuddered and Carter turned to her, his brows pinched together with concern.

"You okay, honey?" His fingers trailed down her arm. "Are you cold? I can get one of my sweatshirts for you."

Easton hopped up from his chair. "I'll do it. It is a cold night."

The sun still wasn't up yet and despite being awake for al-most twenty-four hours Mallory wasn't tired. At least her brain wasn't...her body on the other hand felt like she'd drank far too much caffeine, like when she'd studied for finals back in college. Exhausted and energized all at the same time, her thinking processes sluggish and muddied.

"Thank you."

She didn't want to argue that she wasn't all that cold. It didn't seem polite and these people were only trying to be nice.

Even with Easton out of the room temporarily there were still several pairs of eyes trained on herself and Carter. They all wanted the story and she only hoped she could give it to them. They were a heck of a lot nicer than the police so it ought to be...easier, or at least bearable.

"The tire pressure monitor came on," Carter began. "So I needed to pull over and check the tires. There was a rest stop a mile and a half up. You know, the one between here and Green Pine."

Jason nodded, his fingers stroking his chin. "That's a nice one. Well lit. I always thought it felt safe."

"I did too," Carter agreed grimly. "But clearly we were both wrong. So anyway, I pulled over and Mallory went to the ladies' room as I was finishing up. Then I went too. When I came out, Mallory was leaning over the man and they were both covered in blood."

A simplified version, clean and to the point. And brief. No emotion or commentary. He didn't mention the horror they'd both felt and the sounds the man had made as he'd died.

Jason and his brother West had now turned their attention to Mallory. "Was there anyone else around when you walked outside?"

She shook her head. "No, I didn't see anyone."

West's eyes narrowed. "Just because you didn't see anyone doesn't mean that you were alone."

Well...shit. He had a point.

Now that is truly creepy.

The thought of someone standing in the shadows while she watched the man die was truly awful. Chilling right down to the bone.

Easton returned with a huge dark blue hoodie that zipped up the front. "This should keep you warm."

She accepted it gratefully, feeling chilly after the murderer playing hide and seek talk. She wrapped it around her with a helping hand from Carter. Another point in his favor. She could hardly believe it was the same guy she'd had dinner with.

"The idea that someone might have been watching us freaks me out," Mallory admitted. "That's some creepy stuff right there."

West's lips twisted. "Sorry. I really don't mean to make you afraid. Sometimes I think out loud. I'll try and stop that."

"It's okay, it's just weird. I don't want you to censure yourself because I'm a little queasy about what happened."

West and Jason exchanged a glance before the latter leaned forward in his chair. "Do you think you can tell your story? Right from the beginning? All the details?"

She could, of course. Carter's version had been a good one. Concise and not messy. If they wanted details, it wasn't going to be pretty.

"I can—"

"You don't have to," Carter cut in. "If you don't feel up to it, you don't have to."

Would there be some sort of catharsis if she talked about it to friendly listeners? Or was that simply an optimistic hope?

"I can do that but it's not going to be easy."

Jason looked at Carter. "What about you?"

Carter nodded, his jaw set. "I can but like Mallory told you, this isn't a sweet story."

Jason sat back in his chair. "Then start from the very beginning. What did you see when you pulled into the rest stop? Was there anyone else there?"

Chapter Seven

MALLORY CLOSED HER eyes, her brain sifting through the multitude of images from only hours ago. Some were good, some were neutral, and some were downright horrifying.

"There were other people there," she said. "Carter pulled up in front of the building and parked the car. We both got out to check the tires."

"Was it quiet?" Jason asked. "Or loud? Did you smell anything?"

Olfactory memories. She'd read that they were the most powerful and could last an entire lifetime.

"Nothing out of the ordinary," she replied with a shake of her head. "But it was quiet. Everyone was orderly and minding their own business."

"No, there was a smell," Carter contradicted. "It was leaves. It was faint but I thought I smelled burning leaves."

Her lids fluttered open and she frowned, trying to remember. "Yes, I know what you're talking about. It was so faint, though. Like from a far distance."

"Everything is important," West stated. "Did you tell the police about the smell? There's a small neighborhood a few miles away it could have come from."

"They didn't ask," Carter answered. "They only wanted what we saw."

"Okay," Jason nodded easily. The entire family sat quietly, listening to their stories but not interrupting at all. "What did you see when you got out of the car? Who was there?"

To her relief, Carter replied. "There was a family parked to our right and down the way a few spaces from the victim."

"What kind of car was it?" West asked.

"A minivan." This time it was Mallory who answered. "Maroon. It was a fancy one with the DVD player in the back of the seats so the kids could watch television. A movie I didn't recognize was on but they were asleep."

Thank God they had left before the violence started.

"How many kids?"

"Two. A boy and a girl." She anticipated his next question. "I'm not good with ages, though. Maybe…around ten or twelve? I'm not sure. I didn't get a good look at them and it was dark."

"Would you recognize them if you saw them again?"

Would she? *Could* she?

"No," she said after a long pause. "I just barely glanced at them. I don't think I'd know who they were."

But West didn't stop there. He peppered her with more questions, in far more detail than the cops had asked. Did she remember what the children were wearing? What about shoes? What were the adults wearing?

And on it went. When she couldn't answer, Carter would try but his focus had been on the flat tire and not their surroundings.

"Okay, was there anyone else there?" Jason asked. "Besides the family?"

Carter answered first. "There was also a sedan to our left with a man that was rummaging around in his trunk, along with the vehicle that had pulled in right behind us – a dark-colored Malibu with a female driver."

"It was blue," Mallory added. "Dark blue. And don't forget about the other woman in the SUV. It was silver."

"Right," Carter nodded. "But she was already behind the wheel and left while I was changing the tire."

"She could have come back while you were in the restroom," Jason said. "Or she could have pulled behind the building and turned off her engine and headlights waiting until the other guy was alone."

"She didn't know he'd ever be alone," Mallory pointed out. "No one could possibly know that."

"She could hope," Carter said. "Lie in wait. But I think she left."

"Did you actually see her drive down the ramp to the highway?" West challenged.

"No."

"Then you don't know."

Carter rolled his eyes. "You're being more of a dick than the cops. They just took our stories down and canned the editorial comments. You're not the investigators here."

Easton laughed and stood to refill his coffee. "Since when has that ever stopped them from acting like it?"

West shrugged. "It's a habit. Sue me."

"I'm simply interested in the details of the case," Jason remarked, a smile playing on his lips. "I'm not looking to hunt this guy down. Assuming it's a man."

She'd been thinking about this for hours now. "I think it was the guy who was rummaging in his trunk. That's pretty suspicious behavior, don't you think?"

Carter's brows almost went to his hairline. "No, because I was doing the exact same thing. Do you think I killed him?"

Now he was being a drama king. This was more like the guy she'd had dinner with.

"Of course not."

"Then let's not label any behavior as suspicious." He was silent for a long moment. "Although I kind of agree with you. He never made eye contact with me. The guy with the family did. The mother did. The woman in the Malibu did, but he didn't."

"That's not a sign of guilt," West said. "It could mean many things. Hell, he might be the killer but it doesn't mean anything. Not everyone is as friendly as you are to strangers."

Kathy, who had been quiet this entire time along with Carter's father, elbowed West.

"It might simply be his gut telling him that. Aren't you always talking about a lawman's gut instincts?"

"I am," West readily agreed. "But Carter isn't a lawman."

Peter sat up in his chair and cleared his throat. "He's an Anderson and that means that he's no fool about people."

I'm not so sure about that. He was kind of a jerk tonight.

Carter was rubbing his temples as if he had a headache. "Dad, West has a point."

Peter nodded and then stood up. "Of course, he does. So do you. The fact is none of us know shit. Excuse my language, ladies."

Rock on. I could use a few cuss words myself right about now.

"When you came out of the restroom, Mallory, what happened then?" Jason asked. "Everyone was gone and you were alone."

This. This right here was what she wasn't sure she ready to relive. Those images... She might never sleep again.

She hadn't said a word but Carter, sitting so close their arms were touching, seemed to sense her unrest. He patted her hand underneath the table and then gave it a squeeze.

"I know you all want every detail but I think Mallory is exhausted and frankly, so am I. We need to get a few hours of sleep and then maybe we can resume our discussion about this."

Carter Anderson, you're not a bad guy. You might even be a good one.

Jason winced and rubbed his chin again. "Shit, I'm sorry. Of course, you're exhausted and need some sleep. It's the former agent in me that wants all the details. I really apologize."

Peter slapped Jason on the back. "Both of you should get home to your families. They'll wonder where you are when they wake up."

"Brinley already knows," Jason laughed. "The phone woke her. She has the hearing of a wolf. Any little sound and she's wide awake."

"She has the hearing of a mother," Kathy contradicted. "I'm betting that Gigi knows where West is, too."

His cheeks red, West nodded in agreement. All eyes seemed to turn to Easton who was standing at the counter wolfing down the leftover bacon like a man who hadn't been fed in days.

"What?" he said, chewing and swallowing the mouthful. "Dizzy was blissfully asleep when I left. And if any of you tell her how much bacon and eggs I ate here today I'll totally deny it all and call you a liar. She's got me on a juice cleanse."

Mallory didn't know who Dizzy was but apparently the statement was hilarious because everyone laughed. The party – or whatever this was – was officially breaking up. Everyone stood and the coffee cups were rinsed and placed in the sink. Kathy paused in front of Mallory, her arms held out.

"I know your parents aren't here to give you a hug. May I?"

Mallory wasn't much of a hugger. At least, her family hadn't been. Her parents loved her, she knew that without a doubt, but physical affection wasn't something they displayed often.

Do I want a hug? Yes, I think I do. It can't hurt.

Mallory opened her own arms and was wrapped in a lovely but gentle hug. And yes, it felt better. Human contact was good and what she needed. Her stress level dropped slightly, although she was still tense and agitated. There probably weren't enough hugs to get her to completely relax and forget.

Carter's family filtered out, climbed into their cars, and drove away just as the sun was beginning to peak over the horizon. She'd been up a full twenty-four hours and she felt like a walking zombie.

Closing and locking the door behind him, Carter pressed a few buttons on the wall panel and the security system green light came on.

"Let's get you to bed."

Interesting statement. Earlier this evening it would have been a giant warning sign about a womanizing blind date. Now?

It sounded hopeful but in a completely different way. She'd never sleep again.

Chapter Eight

CARTER HAD TRIED to sleep but that had been a futile effort. Every time he'd tried to close his eyes, he'd think about what he'd seen. It played out like a movie in his mind, and it was so fucking real. The sounds, the smells, even the colors seemed brighter and more vivid. It was as if he was reliving it over and over, forced to watch when there was nothing he could do to stop it. Eventually he'd given up and headed into the kitchen to put on a pot of coffee.

He'd stopped by the guest room where he'd put Mallory and opened the door just a crack to check on her. She probably wouldn't be all that happy about him doing it but he was worried. She'd experienced even more than he had and she'd clearly been shaken up by it. The entire time they'd spent talking to his family, he could feel the tension radiating from her slight frame. She'd been holding it together, but barely.

Luckily, she had fallen asleep at some point probably from sheer exhaustion. When he'd looked in on her, her eyes were closed and her long dark hair was strewn across the white pillowcase like a halo. But sadly, her rest wasn't peaceful. Her breathing had been fast and shallow as her fingers clutched at the sheets. For a moment, he thought about waking her but then changed his mind. Rotten sleep was better than no sleep at all.

He'd ended up in the kitchen, sipping coffee and staring out of the window. Not much was happening outside. A few birds and some squirrels for Tiger to bark at but even the canine had lost interest and had laid down on his favorite cushion by the fireplace and was taking a nap. Carter was alone with his thoughts, a state that he usually avoided as much as possible.

Matthew Montgomery.

Carter hadn't known the man, and now never would, but he'd been a real person with a real life. Like so many, Montgomery had hopes and dreams, plans for the future. He had people that loved him, maybe even someone waiting at home for him. That was all gone. In just a few seconds, everything had changed.

Introspection wasn't a thing that came naturally to Carter. He didn't spend much of his time pondering the questions of the universe or any of his life decisions. He was basically a man of action, preferring deeds over words. But this had turned him around and pulled him inside out. Matthew Montgomery's life was over. Carter was still alive.

But what the fuck was he doing with his life? Sure, he worked hard, busting his ass every day to make the family more money when they really didn't need it. He built things and that had always been satisfying for him. Structures that would still be standing long after he was gone, even if it was only a condo or an office. It was still permanent and a sign he'd been there.

Other people had children as a legacy, Carter had buildings. And what about kids? He wanted a couple, although he hadn't much thought about when. Most of his friends had settled down and were starting families but until recently he'd been content to taste the nectar of as many women as he possibly could. Variety was fun and monogamy was the enemy. He'd turned thirty-three six months ago and he was finding that his taste in entertainment and people were beginning to change.

He'd rather spend a quiet evening at home, maybe watching a movie and cooking dinner. He didn't want to whoop it up with his friends at some loud, smoky honkytonk until closing time and then drag his ass out of bed in the morning. Usually next to a woman he could barely remember. He didn't know who he was becoming or what he wanted out of life but he sure as shit didn't want to be that guy... The one that was older and kind of creepy, hitting on girls in their twenties. No one wanted to be him, least of all Carter.

That was one of the reasons he'd agreed to go on this blind date with Mallory. Someone who didn't hang out in bars or know much about the Anderson family. For one night at least, he could just be himself with a person who didn't have any expectations.

But he wasn't getting any younger and the clock on the wall was ticking away. Montgomery had found that out. There were no guarantees. Carter had to wake the fuck up and stop walking blindly through his life, instead grabbing it by the balls and making it his bitch. If he wanted something he had to make it happen. No putting it off for another day. That day might never come.

"Is there more coffee?"

So lost in his maudlin thoughts, Carter hadn't heard Mallory join him in the kitchen. He swung his feet down from where he had them propped on a chair and hopped up to pour her a cup. "There is. Cream and sugar?"

Rubbing at her eyes, she looked delightfully sleepy. Satin skin with just a flush on her cheeks, hair tumbled from her restless nap, she was completely adorable. Only a thin line of smudged mascara under her eyes gave away that she'd been wearing makeup last night and hadn't had a chance to wipe it off. He'd loaned her a pair of sweatpants and a t-shirt that were far too big and it made it hard to walk. She had to hold up the bottom of the pants as she walked into the kitchen and sat down.

"Cream and two sugars. Thank you. I really need this." She took a sip. "You should have woken me up."

He set the steaming mug in front of her before refilling his own tepid brew.

"I hope you don't mind but I did check on you about an hour ago. You were sleeping and I didn't want to disturb you."

She grimaced and made a face. "I would have welcomed it. I had a nightmare which I guess isn't all that shocking. It would have been a surprise if I didn't. What about you?"

"I never got to sleep, but I'm glad you did. Even if it wasn't peaceful, you needed the rest."

"I'd rather stay awake. In fact, that's the plan for the foreseeable future. What's the record for staying awake?"

He settled in the chair across from her. "I have no idea but I don't think it's a long-term kind of plan. Eventually you'll need to rest. Maybe the doctor can prescribe something for you."

"No way." She shook her head. "I don't like taking anything. When I take cold medicine it gives me weird dreams. I can't imagine what would happen if I took some now. Nothing good,

I bet. What were you doing?"

It was a decent question. Carter was sitting all alone in the kitchen, no radio, no television, and no newspaper. Just sitting.

But he didn't play glib or funny. Better to be honest.

"Thinking. About last night and Montgomery. I would imagine that's what you and I are going to do for awhile."

Wrapping her hands around the warm mug, she nodded. "I guess so. Were you wondering what he was like? I do. I wonder if he had a wife and kids. That would be awful."

The police hadn't told them anything about the victim. He ought to check the news. They'd have all the details.

"I guess something like this just makes you think about your own mortality," he said. "It would probably be strange if it didn't."

They didn't speak for awhile, seemingly content to sip their coffee and stare out of the window. There was still unfinished business between them, however. He'd promised himself that he would apologize.

"If it's not too late...I'd like to apologize about last night. Looking back over the evening, I was a lousy date. I don't have a good excuse but I do have an explanation, if you're open to hearing it."

Her brows raised in question. "I'm listening."

"A buddy of mine from college, his wife went into labor last night in Denver. He was super nervous and kept texting me over and over all the details of what was going on and I was trying to reassure him that it was all normal, although I don't know jackshit about childbirth. He just needed someone to be there for him. They had his wife's family all there but he doesn't have many friends in Denver yet. They just moved there about six months ago. Anyway, that's why I kept getting those texts. I ignored you and that wasn't right. I'm really sorry. I'm usually better on a date."

Mallory seemed to carefully consider his story and then finally nodded. "That's actually a pretty good excuse. Did she have it yet? Was it a boy or a girl?"

"She had the baby about midnight. A boy and thank you for being so nice about it."

A playful smile turned up the corners of her mouth. "Of course that doesn't explain the waitress at dinner."

Fuck.

"Did you know she followed me into the ladies' room at the restaurant?" Mallory asked. "She told me that you were a womanizer and if I was smart I would call a cab and leave you at the table."

Damn. Women were vicious.

"That was Anna. She and I only went out a few times."

"You made quite an impression then."

He didn't know how to explain without sounding like an ass.

"Anna is a nice girl but there was never anything serious between us."

"Did she know that?"

"I hope so," he snorted. "We only went out two or three times. That's hardly a great love affair."

"Did you sleep with her?"

Ah, the million dollar question.

"Does it matter?"

That seemed to amuse Mallory to no end. For the first time

in hours, she was smiling and chuckling, her shoulders shaking with mirth.

"Yes, Carter. It does. You can't go around having sex with women willy-nilly and not have a few consequences. You know…like women thinking they're more important to you than they actually are. Shit happens."

Truer words and all that. Shit did indeed happen, more than he wanted it to.

"Willy-nilly? That's a great phrase. I'm going to work it into my conversations more often."

She placed her hand over her mouth in mock outrage. "Are you making fun of me, Carter Anderson? I'll have you know that I have all sorts of words to replace the bad ones so that I don't cuss in front of my students."

This was pure gold. He had to know more.

"Like what? I may want to use a few on the job sites I visit."

She laughed at that, dimples showing in both cheeks. She really was cute as hell.

"Well…for the f-word, I say fudgesicles."

"Fudgesicles," he repeated dutifully. "That doesn't seem to have the same…impact, but please do go on."

She shrugged. "It's the usual stuff. Fudge nuggets. God bless America. Son of a gun. Jiminy crickets. Bull spit. I even sometimes say gee whiz."

"Beaver and Theodore would be delighted." His smile fell. "I really am sorry about our date. It was all my fault."

"Yes, it was."

She said it so seriously that Carter couldn't contain his laughter. Luckily, she joined in.

"I have to share some of the blame, too," she said. "I could have tried harder but I was a little miffed about your phone going off again and again, and then the whole waitress thing kind of threw me. But I want you to know that it wasn't the worst date I've been on."

That only made him feel marginally better.

"How about we try again?" He held his breath waiting for her response. To his shock, he really wanted her to say yes. He wanted another chance to show her who he could be. "Another date and this time I'll be on my best behavior."

She didn't even hesitate. "Yes. We can do that. I'll try harder, too."

For a long moment they simply stared at one another, both of them smiling like idiots. He cleared his throat to break the tension.

"Should I turn on the television?" He glanced at the clock on the wall. "There might be something about last night on the news."

Even now he was having trouble calling it what it was. A murder.

They both went into the living room and settled on the couch, Tiger at his feet. Carter clicked through the channels until he found the local all-news and weather cable station. The news anchor was talking but the sound was too low. He zoomed it up just as they cut from the studio to footage of the rest stop last night and the sergeant who had tried to separate them. He was being interviewed by the reporter.

The sergeant gave a few details about the case but not too many, being deliberately vague especially when asked about whether there were suspects. Carter was ready to turn the volume down when the station cut to another clip.

This one was of that same reporter talking to him and Mallory. It was startling, seeing himself on the television. Pale and clearly agitated, he barely recognized himself. Sitting next to him, Mallory groaned and covered her eyes.

"Dear God, please tell me that's not actually me on television. What was I thinking? Talking to that reporter…"

"We didn't do it voluntarily, honey. They ambushed us on the way out of the building."

Carter watched as his attorney Bryce insinuated himself between the aggressive reporter and Mallory. Apparently, they'd decided that she looked like a better target for questions than he did so they'd stuck the microphone in her face and wouldn't back off.

She peeked out through her fingers. "Is it over yet? Tell me when it's over. There are zombies that look better than I do."

"It's over." The station had gone back to the studio and the anchor. "Jesus, I hope no one saw that. I don't really want any questions about this from people I barely know. And you looked fine."

His cell immediately buzzed in the pocket of his sweatpants. Then, even from across the room, they could both hear the chime of Mallory's phone as well, tucked away in her purse.

Damn. So much for anonymity and finding a way to move on after last night.

Chapter Nine

M ALLORY HAD TO hand it to Carter. He'd given his all to convince her to stay at his place a little longer. All of his arguments were well-thought out and made a heck of a lot of sense. Especially the one where she'd have more privacy staying at the ranch with him than in her little townhouse in Green Pine. The idea of reporters dogging her heels for creepy details about that poor man's death made her angry but she couldn't hide away forever. Could she?

No, you can't. You have to stand on your own two feet.

It wasn't Carter's job to protect her or manage this situation. She needed to deal with it herself. She had to admit, however, that the ranch had felt safe and far away from the day to day issues.

She hadn't been able to escape her constantly ringing phone though, and it was fast becoming a real nuisance. She didn't know that many people in the area but every single one of them had called or texted her, wanting to know all of the dirty, bloody details firsthand. Poor Carter had been hammered even harder since he knew literally almost everyone in Tremont and beyond, having lived here all of his life.

Her phone was now in silent mode, sitting on the bedside table charging. She gave it a glare as she walked by before grabbing a bath towel from the dryer. She needed to fold some laundry but tomorrow would be good enough. In the meantime, a hot, steamy shower was exactly what she needed to clear the cobwebs from her mind. Carter was picking her up for their second-first-date at six. She had plenty of time to get ready, maybe even take a quick nap if she could fall asleep.

Tossing the towel over her shoulder, she didn't make it all the way to the bathroom. The insistent ring of the doorbell shattered the peace and quiet. Groaning, she hurried toward the door hoping it was only a package delivery or maybe a child selling cookies. She looked out of the peephole and groaned. This was the last thing she needed this afternoon.

Her nosy neighbor Dara was practically laying on the bell, determined not to be ignored. While Mallory liked Dara, she could be long-winded and didn't have a good sense of personal boundaries. She also didn't seem to be able to know when she'd out-stayed her welcome.

Mallory could hide and pretend she wasn't home but her car was in the driveway. She also wasn't fond of being a hostage in her own house. If she needed to go anywhere later, she'd have to try and sneak out. But this conversation was inevitable. The only question was when it was going to take place.

Just get it over with.

Pulling the door open, Mallory painted a smile on her face. "Hello, Dara. I wasn't expecting to see you today. Carl didn't have a soccer game?"

Dara's husband Carl played indoor soccer almost every single weekend. The couple looked to be in their mid-thirties and had been married almost two years. They were always friendly and nice but since Dara had been laid off from her administrative assistant job last month, she'd become the neighborhood gossip. She was constantly watching other people's business and then wanting to talk about it. Mallory took a much more live-and-let-live approach to those around her so she didn't want to discuss whether Mrs. Abernathy could afford that new luxury car or not. It wasn't any of Mallory's business. She wasn't making the payments.

The pretty brunette nodded and then shook her head as if she wasn't sure. "He does have a game but I told him to go without me. After we saw you on the news today, I knew I had to talk to you. Oh my gosh, are you alright? Everybody has been so worried. You could have been killed, you know."

Thanks, I did know that but I appreciate the reminder.

Everybody had been worried? Just how many people had Dara spoken to?

"I'm fine." Mallory tried to make her voice sound as reassuring as possible, although her psyche wasn't as sure that all was well. "It's sweet of you to worry about me but I'm okay. It was scary but I'll be fine."

So we're all fine.

Mallory hadn't budged from the doorway but Dara was looking over her shoulder and into the living room. What was she looking for? Clearly she wanted to be invited in.

"You didn't come home last night," Dara observed, standing on her tiptoes to peer farther into the house. "And then a man brought you home. He was pretty handsome. He was the one on television too, wasn't he?"

One didn't have to be a genius to see where Dara was taking this. If she'd been watching, she had to know that Carter hadn't stuck around but perhaps she was hoping to find evidence that a man was staying there.

"He was," Mallory confirmed. "We spent most of the night giving our statements to the police, and then he brought me home."

It wasn't any of Dara's business what happened in between, and Mallory wasn't inclined to give any details.

"That must have been so frightening." Dara reached out and patted Mallory on the arm. "I could make you some tea, if you like. You must be exhausted."

That was an understatement. But Dara still wasn't going to be invited in. Mallory had learned this lesson already. Her friendly neighbor would settle in and it might be hours before she could be pried out of one of the kitchen chairs and back to her own house.

Mallory stood her ground, not moving from her spot nor opening the door any wider. She absolutely, positively without a shadow of a doubt didn't want to discuss last night with this woman. "Actually, I was just about to get in the shower. Maybe another time?"

Dara's mouth turned down almost into a pout but it quickly turned into a charming smile.

"That's perfect. I can fix you some tea while you shower."

Persistence, thy name is Dara.

"I have a lot to do, I'm afraid. I need to call my family too."

All the way in Florida they wouldn't have heard about this but Mallory wanted them to hear it from her before they saw it on CNN, should the case go national for some crazy reason.

"I–I'm just so worried about you. Everybody is. You shouldn't be alone at a time like this. If your family lived closer I'm sure they'd be here."

They would be and it would be lovely. But they were family. Dara was not.

The one thing Mallory had learned growing up in a house with two sisters and a brother, and then with three roommates in college, was that she had to have boundaries with people. She was no stranger to putting them up and she had no trouble enforcing them.

"I can't talk about it," Mallory said flatly. "I know you'll understand and respect that."

She'd let Dara figure out if the reason she couldn't talk about it was because the cops didn't want her to or because she simply didn't want to discuss it.

"Well…of course. I totally respect that."

But clearly don't like it.

"Thank you. I really do appreciate you coming to check on me. We have such a wonderful neighborhood here. I feel very lucky."

Mallory did, indeed, feel fortunate. So far everyone she'd talked to in their little townhouse development was as friendly as could be. That didn't mean she owed them all the dark and bloody details from last night.

Disappointed, Dara finally turned and walked back across the street, although this probably wasn't going to be her one and only try. She'd regroup and be back, maybe with brownies.

Closing and locking her door, Mallory heaved a relieved sigh. She hadn't wanted it to get ugly but she wasn't going to be a pushover, either. She'd been through a traumatic event last night but she wasn't going to allow herself to get bogged down in it. She had to pick herself up and get on with life. The best way to start that seemed like a cleansing shower. She might not be over what she'd witnessed but she'd be clean. Not a bad way to face the world.

✦   ✦   ✦

GIVEN A SECOND chance at a first date, Carter wasn't about to blow it. He arrived at Mallory's door on time and holding a big bouquet of flowers. He was going to be the luckiest man in Tremont tonight because she looked amazing. Dressed for the chillier weather, she was wearing a red sweater dress that clung to every curve and brown suede boots that made her slightly taller. He'd still have to bend down to kiss her but not quite as far. She'd left her hair loose around her shoulders and his fingers itched to reach out and run his fingers through the long, silky strands. He'd been an idiot last night to ignore this woman.

His brothers and cousins were right. He was stupid as hell. But he intended to fix that immediately.

"They're beautiful," Mallory exclaimed as she ushered him in. She accepted the flowers and sniffed at them delicately. "They smell like heaven. This was so thoughtful. Thank you, Carter."

He hadn't thought they would bring her such pleasure but he was damn glad he'd decided to buy them. It had been something of an impulse purchase.

"You're welcome. I'm glad you like them. I want tonight to go better than last night."

He followed her into the kitchen as she fished a vase out of a cabinet and filled it with water.

"Considering how crappy last night was, the bar isn't very high," she remarked, arranging the multi-colored bouquet. Suddenly she stopped and turned to him, her eyes narrowed suspiciously. "Do you buy flowers for women a lot?"

He didn't take offense at the question. With his reputation it was a fair query, and he respected the hell out of her for asking it.

"I can't remember the last time I bought flowers for a woman," he answered honestly. "Hell, it may have been a corsage for my high school prom."

"Really?" She appeared to be surprised. "Wow, that's a long time in between posies."

He didn't say it out loud but he hadn't had to buy females flowers. His money had been lure enough.

His phone went off again and he grimaced, pulling it from his pocket and checking the caller. No one he wanted to speak to. He pressed the decline button with a growl of frustration.

"It is not going to happen again tonight, I promise you. We are not going to have our date interrupted every five seconds by my phone."

"Is it your buddy again? Is everything okay?"

He held up the offending piece of technology. "It's everyone I've ever known, talked to, or even passed by on the street calling about last night. They all want the story from me and they all think they're the first person to have the completely original idea to contact me to get it. I'm ready to chuck this out of a window, although that wouldn't stop them. I've been accosted at the grocery store and the local gas station."

"I get it. Mine hasn't been as crazy as yours because I don't know too many people here, but the few that I do have all called. I even had the neighbor across the street come over on the pretense of making me tea but I know she wanted to get the inside scoop." Mallory nodded toward her purse on the kitchen island. "I talked to my parents earlier so I just shut the thing off and put it away."

"I know a few quiet restaurants around here where I don't think we'll be hassled too much."

Mallory tapped her chin in thought. "You know, we don't have to go out. We could just order a pizza and watch some television here."

That would be awesome but he didn't want her to think he was a cheapskate or that he was too lazy to plan a date.

"I'd like that but...I'm happy to take you out."

Her eyes sparkled and she leaned in closer so he caught a whiff of her perfume. "I'll tell you a secret if you keep it to yourself. I'm kind of a homebody and after last night and this morning, an evening at home sounds like heaven."

It really did and he was grateful she'd suggested it.

"Pepperoni."

She frowned and shook her head. "Pardon?"

"I like pepperoni on my pizza. How about you?"

She smiled and his heart beat a little bit faster. "Sausage with double cheese."

"I can get behind that, especially the double cheese part."

Tonight was going to be much better than last night. No doubt about it.

Chapter Ten

C ARTER PATTED HIS stomach and pushed away his empty
plate. He and Mallory had just spent the last hour sitting
on the floor and eating pizza while swapping stories from their
childhood. Hers had been pretty standard but she had many of
the same issues he did, coming from a large family and being the
youngest. Separating, creating one's own identity. Her move
here had been a part of that. There was something more though
that she wasn't as forthcoming about. He could tell the way she
paused every now and then, choosing her words with such
extreme care.

"My parents didn't want me to take this teaching job," she
confessed with a grimace. "But I needed a big change."

"How is it going so far?"

She stood and gathered the plates to take into the kitchen,
her stocking clad feet soundless on the hardwood floors. She'd
changed into jeans and a sweater earlier when they'd decided to
stay in for the evening. "Pretty well until last night. I had the
blind date from hell."

It was good they could kind of laugh about it because if they
really thought it through they'd be either screaming or crying. A

sense of humor was one of the most attractive things about a female. Brains were right up there, too.

"I bet he was really a nice guy," Carter said in mock protest. "It probably wasn't his fault."

The dishes clattered in the sink and Mallory rolled her eyes. "He was on his phone all night."

"That is rude."

"I know."

"Unless he had a really good reason."

She came back and sprawled next to him on their mound of cushions. "You sound like you're on his side."

"I'm not taking sides."

She sniffed disdainfully. "All you men stick together."

It was the way she said it... The words came out of his mouth before he could stop them.

"It sounds like you know that from experience."

Her smile vanished and he could hear the sharp intake of her breath. He'd hit a nerve.

"You could say that."

He didn't think she was going to say anything else which was fine. None of this was frankly any of his damn business but then she continued, deliberately not looking at him but some far off place at some time in the past.

"I was with someone for a long time. I thought we were going to get married."

Oh shit. He'd opened up a can of worms and he wanted to slap himself repeatedly on the head. This was going to be bad. So very awful.

But then to his surprise she turned to face him, their gazes colliding. "Turns out he spent the last year of our relationship cheating on me. When I found out I ended things. It wasn't so much that I was heartbroken, I know that now. I don't think I loved him the way I was supposed to and I'm guessing it was the same for him. I do think he should have manned up and admitted he didn't want to be in the relationship anymore, though. He was a coward and I could never be with someone like that."

"It must have been difficult."

Wow, what a pathetic comment. I suck at this.

"What was difficult was realizing that I'd been living in my own little fantasy land. I was going to marry my college boyfriend and live happily ever after. We'd have an amazing wedding, then buy a house, and have two kids and a dog."

"Don't forget the minivan."

Can I just shut my mouth?

Mallory didn't take offense, instead laughing at his remark. "We can't forget that, can we? I was so busy planning my perfect future I neglected to notice that I didn't have the right man. We'd been growing apart for some time."

"Do you still want the house and the dog?" he felt compelled to ask. "And the two kids?"

She shook her head, her smile growing bigger. If she'd been heartbroken at one point, she wasn't anymore. "No, I just want to be happy whether it's in a relationship or out of it. That's why I was of two minds about going on the blind date to begin with. I wasn't sure that I really wanted a man in my life, to be honest. What about you? What do you want?"

What did he want? That was an excellent question. Until recently he would have said that he wanted to have fun and be with beautiful women. Lots of them.

Been there, done that.

Lately he'd been wondering if there was something more out there. He'd watched as brothers and cousins tied the knot and now only he and Noah were holdouts. They seemed happy and content, happier than they'd been when they were single. They were building families and homes and if there was one thing Carter admired that was *building something.*

"I'm not sure," he replied slowly, his mind still whirring with too many thoughts but no conclusions. "I know that I've always wanted a relationship like my parents but frankly I haven't done a thing towards getting that. Quite the opposite, actually."

Her head tilted and she studied him for a long moment as if she could see inside of his head. "Would you call yourself a womanizer, Carter? Because you…have a reputation."

One he'd worked hard to get. It was only as he grew older that he'd realized that people didn't always agree that he had something to be proud of.

Back to the question…

"Yes," he admitted. "I am, or at least I was. I'm not sure that I can be called that anymore or that I even want to be. It was fun when I was younger but honestly, I'm getting to the point where I don't want to spend my Friday and Saturday nights in a loud, smelly bar and then waking up feeling like shit the next day. That's a young man's game."

"Waking up with a different woman," she said shrewdly, her lips pursed. "That was part of the *game* too, right?"

Wincing at his unfortunate choice of words, he nodded in agreement. No point in trying to pretend because he'd been a real shit. "I'm not proud of a lot of my behavior but I never pretended with a woman that I was anything but who I was. If they got any other ideas, it wasn't from me. I've been screaming from the rooftops since I was a teenager that I wanted to play the field and not get tied down with one woman."

It didn't really make it any better, though. He still sounded like a real douche bag.

"Women very often think they can change a man. I blame fairy tales, movies, and love songs."

"I don't think the *Die Hard* series is to blame for societal ills, Mallory."

Laughing, she threw up her hands. "That movie isn't so innocent, either."

"I guess I've kind of been a jerk with women."

"Probably some women," she agreed, her expression solemn now. "The ones that didn't understand the rules of your game or the ones that thought if they loved you enough it would make you want whatever they did. Perhaps even the women that started out just looking for fun but then they fell for you despite their best intentions. But you didn't do the things you did all by yourself. You did have some female cooperation along the way. The big question is—who do you want to be now and in the future?"

"That's what I don't know," he replied lamely, fiddling with the soda can he'd drained a while ago. "I don't want to be that guy anymore but I'm not sure I'm ready for a family and a white picket fence."

"Don't forget the minivan," Mallory teased, a smile playing around the corners of her full mouth. "Seriously, there has to be some space in the middle of those two extremes. At least I hope there is because that's where I think I'd like to be right now. I'm not ready for a wedding dress but I'm past just wanting to date around."

It was a relief to know that Mallory wasn't looking for a diamond ring and forever. For the first time in a long time with a woman, Carter didn't feel the pressure he usually did. She wasn't looking to land a husband or an Anderson.

They were both looking for romance and this conversation had suddenly become far too serious. It was time to lighten it up a smidge.

"There is one thing I know I want," he said, leaning forward so their faces were close together. "Something that, frankly, I've been thinking about since you opened your front door to me that first time last night."

Her pupils were blown wide, her lips parted in anticipation. This was the dance. As old as time, their bodies knew what was happening even if their brains hadn't quite caught up. The tension built between them, but it was delicious and heady. He breathed in deeply, filling his lungs with her intoxicating scent. This woman had no idea just how desirable she was.

"What have you been thinking about?"

The words came out almost as a whisper, their gazes never wavering from one another. Blood roared in his ears and pumped through his veins like a freight train. He couldn't remember the last time he'd been this attracted to a woman. And if he was reading her signals right, she was attracted to him, too.

"Kissing you."

He wasn't sure which one of them made the first move, but

within seconds their lips were touching. Pulling her closer, he ran his fingers down her spine, delighting in the shiver he could feel run through her body. He ran his tongue softly over her bottom lip and she opened to him, deepening the kiss until they were a tangle of arms and legs on the rug.

Her own hands weren't idle, however. One hand stroked the back of his neck while the other gripped his shoulder as if for dear life. Dragging his lips from hers, he pressed kisses over her satiny jaw as his fingers found the warm bare skin of her lower back where her sweater had ridden up. Mallory tasted like tomatoes, garlic, red wine, and something else that he couldn't put his finger on. Only she had it and he was quickly becoming addicted.

He nipped at her ear lobe and then ran his tongue down her neck to where her pulse beat frantically. He took in another lungful of her scent and before capturing her lips again, but this time the kiss was different. Before it had been an exploration. A beginning. This was more but what he couldn't say. He only knew he couldn't get enough.

He didn't know how long they lay there, tasting, touching, exploring. There were sighs, moans, and even a few giggles at one point when he'd found a particularly ticklish spot at her waist. His body was hard and ready, the heat searingly hot between them. The sex was going to be off the charts amazing.

A hand pressed against his shoulder and he lifted up, tearing his mouth from hers. Her lips were swollen and her long dark hair was tousled around her head. Both of them were breathing heavy, panting loudly in the silence.

Fuck, she was gorgeous. He wanted nothing more than to

sweep her into his arms and carry her into the bedroom, making love to her all night long. But a voice in the back of his head kept him from doing just that. He'd been wanting to make a change in his life. He might not be sure how to do that but one thing was for sure…

Doing the same thing over and over and expecting a different result was the definition of insanity.

Add into that the fact that Mallory was looking unsure. She was holding back, caution in those expressive eyes. There was passion and desire to be sure but it was tempered with a dash of fear. After the story she'd told him about her cheating ex-boyfriend she might not be ready to give him all of her trust.

"I think…maybe we should slow down," she finally said, breaking the silence.

The crossroad was clear in front of Carter. He could go down the familiar path, doing what had felt right and natural for years but had become less and less satisfying over time, or he could take the unknown road. This wouldn't make him a different person and it didn't guarantee an outcome. He might fuck this all up no matter which way he went.

It wasn't the end of the world if he didn't get laid tonight. Or tomorrow night.

But let's not make this a habit.

Chapter Eleven

MALLORY HELD HER breath, waiting for Carter's reaction. There was a fifty-fifty shot that he'd get up and leave. Other men had, although to be fair, some had stayed. She'd simply never been the type to jump into bed with a guy right away. She was attracted to Carter, but her innate cautious nature wouldn't let her slide between the sheets with someone she'd only known a little more than twenty-four hours.

It wasn't his reputation, although that would have been enough to make most women wary. She simply didn't get naked with a man on the first date.

Or the second first date. Even if he was as sexy and funny as Carter Anderson.

"Okay," he finally responded, drawing the word out so it sounded as if it were two syllables. "That's fine. I wasn't assuming."

But he was. She could see it in his eyes. He'd thought they were off to the races, rolling around on her living room floor. For a moment, she'd been lost to the pleasure and she'd almost succumbed to his practiced technique. This man knew how to kiss and touch. He was a pro at seduction, knowing just what to do and when to do it. She could see why he was so successful with the ladies.

"I'm not saying that I don't find you attractive because I do." She was explaining too much now, her mouth moving without the benefit of a speed bump of judgment between it and her brain. "Very attractive. It's just that I don't go around hopping into bed with men I just met. I mean…I know that we've been through something traumatic together, but that doesn't mean…Shit. I'm rambling, aren't I?"

He sat up and grinned, his hair askew where she'd run her fingers through the silky strands.

Do not think about how good it felt. Don't go there.

"You are rambling, but it's cute."

She highly doubted that for a second. She was well on her way to *blithering idiot* if she didn't get herself under control. His kisses had sent her into a spin and she wasn't thinking straight.

"I just want you to under–"

"I get it," Carter cut in. "I didn't expect us to go to bed together. Sure, I *hoped* we would. Hell to the yes, I want to, but believe it or not I'm not that spoiled. I don't assume that every woman is going to fall into bed and her panties dissolve with just my mere manly presence."

For some reason that struck Mallory as funny. She had an icky vision of a pair of panties dissolving into a pile of goo on the floor while serenely making conversation during dinner at a nice restaurant.

Carter, on the other hand, had no clue why she was giggling, her hand over her mouth. He was staring at her like she'd completely lost her mind and perhaps she had.

Hiccupping, she tried to explain. "It's just the image. Dissolving panties. It's so gross and funny at the same time."

"You have a strange sense of humor, Mallory Cook."

"You have no idea."

A grin spread across his face. "I like it. It's a little twisted. Like mine."

Were they two peas in a pod? Only time would tell, of course. He had been described as over the top.

"My siblings think I'm weird."

"So do mine," he confided. "It's a badge of honor, honey. You certainly don't want to be normal, do you?"

At one point she might have but she didn't anymore. This was far too much fun.

"No, but I am sorry."

"What for? Saying no? Cock blocking me after some pizza? It's certainly not how any guy wants the evening to end but I'll survive." He frowned, his brows pulled down. "Damn, did I say cock block? I'm sorry. I didn't mean to say that in front of a lady."

She was laughing again and having the best time with this man. She was very glad she'd said yes to this blind date, and then said yes again to a second first date.

"You're fine," she waved away his concerns. "You should hear some of the things my students say. They'd turn your ears blue."

"Honey, they wouldn't turn my ears blue. I probably invented half of those curse words."

"Braggart."

He waggled his eyebrows. "I have mad skills, babe. Just wait and see."

Slapping her hand over her mouth, she shook with laughter. He was a goofball, too. Good. He didn't take himself too seriously. That was an attractive quality in a man.

"Do you have the skills to pick out a movie that we can watch?"

His gaze ran over her small DVD collection. "I do. I bet you like romantic comedies."

That explained the film from last night. She needed to set him straight before they saw all of Meg Ryan's movies.

"I hate them. I actually like action films. I have the whole *Die Hard* series. You did mention it."

A huge smile spread across his face. "Woman, you are perfect."

She wasn't but it was sure nice to have a man around that thought she was.

✦　✦　✦

BRUCE WILLIS HAD saved the world, and Mallory and Carter had raided the ice cream in her freezer. They'd eaten every bite before tossing the empty carton in the trash, both of them feeling a little guilty about the amount of junk food they'd consumed in one evening. It had been a great second first date but all good things had to come to an end, and Mallory found herself walking Carter to his car around midnight.

She'd wrapped a sweater around her shoulders but the cool night air hit her hard and made her shiver. Carter immediately noticed and placed his arm around her waist, pulling her close to his warm body.

I could get used to this.

When they reached his vehicle, she leaned against the door and looked up at him. Despite the porch light, his face was bathed in shadow giving him almost a mysterious look that he quickly ruined by grinning happily. Carter Anderson wasn't *mystery man* material but he was a heck of a lot of fun.

Bracing his hand on the roof of the car, he leaned down and pressed his lips to hers. The kiss was soft and slow and so delicious it made her toes curl in her shoes. It ended far too soon but he didn't move away, their faces inches apart. She could smell the citrus of his body wash and feel his warm breath on her cheek. The heat of his body chased away the cold and she had to fight the urge to *get closer.* Her body was all full speed ahead but her brain and heart were holding up caution flags.

"Why don't you join us for Sunday dinner tomorrow?" he asked. "I forgot to ask you earlier. My mom suggested it but I think it's a great idea. She and Dad want to make sure that you're okay, and frankly, you don't want to miss her famous lasagna. It's legendary in Tremont."

That sounded…intimate. A family dinner. So soon?

"The Anderson Sunday dinners are an experience not to be missed," Carter went on. "Usually most or all of the family is there and it gets pretty loud. My brothers and cousins can be real asses but they're good guys, and their wives are sweet. There's kids too, so I hope that doesn't bother you."

It didn't. She was a teacher and she liked children. It actually sounded sort of wonderful but she wasn't sure this was a good idea.

"I don't want to intrude. It sounds like a family event."

"Mom specifically invited you. We have people over all the time. If you don't go, she'll just stalk you until you give in. You'll end up having coffee with her or lunch. She's worried about you."

It was nice to be worried about. Mallory's parents were concerned as well but they were a long way away and couldn't be right there to comfort her when she needed it. No sense crying over the circumstances, though. She'd known that she'd be on her own here. In a way, it had been part of the allure.

She realized she'd been quiet a long time. He was watching her wrestle with the decision and probably wondering why it was so hard. It was just a meal. It wasn't tea with the Queen of England.

"Can I let you know in the morning?"

Such a cop out. Meeting the family was a big step in most relationships. Carter wasn't like most men, though.

"Sure," he nodded, straightening up and dropping his hand to his side. "I'll call you. Now go inside and lock the door behind you. I'm going to stay out here and make sure you do."

This protective side of Carter was extremely attractive. He was kind of bossy too, but she could deal with it.

"I had a good time tonight," she said a little shyly, looking up at him from under her lashes. "Thank you for the pizza."

"Thank you for the ice cream and the movies. I had a lot of fun." He leaned down and brushed his lips across hers, making her ache for more. "Sweet dreams, Mallory."

Pulling the sweater tighter around her torso, she walked away immediately missing his warmth. When she closed the front door behind her and clicked the lock shut, she looked out of the window where he was standing. Watching. Just as he'd said he would. He turned and climbed into his vehicle and drove out of sight, his red taillights disappearing last.

Closing the drapes, Mallory kicked off her shoes and padded on stocking feet to her bedroom. She would definitely dream of Carter tonight.

Chapter Twelve

THE LOUD BANGING on Carter's front door woke him up the next morning, the sun barely over the horizon. There were only a few people brave enough to drag his ass out of bed at this hour. His mom and dad, of course. Travis, his cousin, who was long past giving any fucks. And Noah, his older brother and a real pain in the butt.

Noah. He better have a damn good reason for this.

"What the hell do you want?" Carter growled when he opened the door, jeans on, barefoot, and shirtless. Tiger was already in the kitchen waiting on breakfast. "In some states I could shoot you for disturbing my peace."

"Go ahead. You're so bleary-eyed you couldn't hit the broad side of barn right now. You need coffee."

"Did you bring any?" Carter shot back as he closed the door behind them, but Noah was already headed into the kitchen.

"No, but I know how to make some. You're such a bear in the morning. Jesus, I feel sorry for the woman that gets stuck with you. She won't want to come near you until after eight."

Noah ran the ranch and that meant he was up long before the sun or the chickens. It was a good fit because he was disgustingly happy in the morning. He loved it. He was constantly going on and on about how great it was to get up before everyone else and how peaceful and quiet it was.

Carter liked mornings too, but after growing up on a ranch and doing chores when it was still dark and freezing outside he enjoyed the hell out of sleeping late in his nice warm bed.

"Most civilized people don't get up at four-thirty in the morning." Carter checked his phone and winced. "It's only seven. I didn't get to bed until one."

Noah slapped a filter into the basket of the coffeemaker. "Early to bed and early to rise. Were you out with Mallory?"

Instantly on his guard, Carter tensed at his brother's question. Something was going on. He didn't know what it was but his brothers rarely showed up at his house at the buttcrack of dawn and asked him about the current woman in his life.

"I was. Why?"

Might as well stop the dancing and get to the damn point.

Carter filled Tiger's food bowl and freshened up the water. Might as well make the pup happy this morning. Someone ought to be.

Noah shrugged and pressed the start button on the coffeemaker. "Just asking. Is that a crime?"

Crossing his arms over his chest, Carter leaned a hip against the kitchen counter. "Since when do you care about my love life?"

His brother opened his mouth to answer and then snapped it shut. Taking a breath, he rubbed the back of his neck and sighed.

"Okay, you've got me on that one. Listen, I've been sort of

deputized to talk to you."

Yep, nothing good was going to come from this.

"About?" Carter prompted. "I'm waiting with bated breath to hear what you all think I need to be told."

As the youngest male, he'd been lectured by his brothers and cousins more times than he could count. About women, about cars, about careers, about money, about…shit in general. He was beginning to lose patience with it all.

"It's not like that." Noah shook his head but seemed less sure of himself than he had only a few moments ago. "We just want to make sure that you don't mess things up with this woman. She seems like a real keeper and those don't come around often, bro."

Whenever Noah called him *bro*, he knew some fuckery was afoot. Were Mom and Dad a part of this, too?

"Just who is *we?*"

"You know, all of us."

"You sat around and talked about me? Christ, you must lead the most boring lives. Get a hobby, big brother. I hear the local women's council is putting on a production of *The Sound of Music*. Maybe you could get a part as one of the Von Trapp kids."

Noah appeared unfazed by Carter's vitriol. "We're just worried about you."

"Really? That's kind of funny, because they're not worried about you. You're way older than me and you aren't any closer to finding the love of your life than I am. Hell, at least I'm dating. When was the last time you went out with a woman? Do you even remember what to do with one?"

This time his brother's cheeks turned a ruddy shade. "Vague-ly, but honestly I don't have time to find a woman. I'm busy running the ranch and that takes every hour of the day. She'd have to show up on the doorstep for me to meet someone." He poked himself in the chest and then pointed to Carter. "But I'm not you. We've all seen your increasing dissatisfaction with your life and Mallory is your chance to change things."

Carter was well aware of what was going on in his own damn life.

"And you all think I'm so fucking pathetic that I'm going to blow it? Is that about right? You think that I need to be told what to do so that Mallory doesn't go running into the moun-tains to get away from me."

Noah held up his hands in surrender. "Hell, no. We just want to see you happy."

"Whatever you think happy is." Carter pushed away from the counter and stomped over to his brother, getting nose to nose, his hands clenched in fists at his side. Tiger whined and scooted closer to his leg, sensing the tension in the room. "This shit stops now. I am so fucking tired of every one of you having an opinion about what I need to do with my life and career. Every fucking one of you told me where to go to college, what to major in, what kind of car to drive, and what sports to play. Hell, you even have an opinion about what beer I should drink. Most of the time I just tune you all out and then turn around and do whatever the hell I want but I've grown tired of you all thinking that you have a say in how I run my life. You don't. Not at all. Step back and fuck off. I'll run my life any goddamn way I want to."

Noah's eyes were wide and he appeared stunned, as if he'd been hit in the head by a ball that came out of nowhere and his brain hadn't caught up to it yet. Slowly a smile spread across his face which only served to piss Carter off even more. This wasn't funny, dammit.

"Holy shit, little brother. Sounds like you're all grown up."

Son of a bitch. Carter was this close to throwing a punch right in Noah's face.

"I have been for awhile, genius, you just didn't notice. Now stay out of my life or I'll rearrange that pretty face of yours."

That simply made Noah laugh. "You do realize that my pretty face is damn near the same as yours? Now seriously, tell me about your date with Mallory. How did it go? We all really liked her."

Carter liked her, too. He simply didn't know what that meant yet.

Chapter Thirteen

T HE GORGEOUS RED roses in a lovely vase were sitting on
Mallory's welcome mat the next morning, right next to her
newspaper. Smiling, she carried them inside, enjoying the heady
fragrance of the flowers. A small card poked up from between
the buds and she tugged it out of the envelope to read it.

Thank you for a lovely evening. Can't wait to see you again.

Carter hadn't signed it but then he didn't need to. She
shouldn't be so happy about a dozen roses but they were simply
so beautiful and smelled like heaven. He'd admitted that buying
bouquets wasn't something he did usually so that made it all the
more special.

That doesn't mean he thinks I'm special, though.

Mallory needed to keep her head on straight. Falling for
Carter Anderson would be so easy. He was handsome, charming,
funny, intelligent, and kind of goofy. He was – in a nutshell –
just her type. The problem was he was many women's type. She
wasn't someone who wanted to compete for a man.

All day her anticipation built as those flowers kept catching
her eye. They brought back steamy memories of last night that
made it hard to concentrate on the papers she was trying to

grade. The kisses, the caresses, the desire he hadn't bothered to hide. It had been a long time since she'd felt so wanted. In a small way she had missed being in a relationship and not just because of the sex. That was part of it but it was also nice to have a partner to share things with. Talk about their day, go see movies, share a funny story. Most of the time Mallory was fine on her own but every now and then it would be nice to have a man around.

Men snore. Drop their socks on the floor. Leave the toilet seat up.

It would be better to be realistic. No romanticizing what it would be like to have Carter in her life.

That didn't mean she couldn't look nice, though. She spent a few extra minutes in front of the bathroom mirror making sure her hair was under control and her makeup wasn't too garish. She was going for the *no makeup makeup look* which took more products than one would think. She was gliding on her lipgloss when the doorbell chimed. Right on time.

Smoothing down her sweater with her damp palms, she took a deep breath before opening the door. Damn, he looked amazing. Like herself, he was dressed casually in denim but there was something about a man in well-fitting jeans. Mallory couldn't articulate exactly what that something was but it was making it hard to speak.

His face split into a grin. "You look gorgeous. Are you ready to go?"

Miraculously, the gift of speech came back along with a warm, tingly feeling from his compliment. "I am. Come on in while I put on my coat."

He stepped in but stayed by the door so she had to point out the roses on the coffee table.

"Thank you, by the way. They're absolutely beautiful. It was so thoughtful and sweet of you to send them."

Frowning, he walked in close enough to reach out and touch a petal. "Was there a card?"

He didn't look happy. Were they not what he ordered? Maybe he'd asked for a different flower or vase.

"There was." She slipped into her coat and then retrieved the card and envelope from the kitchen counter. "Here. Did they mess up the order?"

He read the card and then looked back at the flowers. "I didn't send these, honey. I wish to hell that I had, but I didn't. Looks like you have a secret admirer."

Wait…what? That didn't make any sense.

"I hardly know anyone here," she stuttered, shocked at his words. "I just assumed… I mean, the card mentioned last night."

Carter snapped his teeth together, his jaw tight. "I noticed that and I don't like it one bit. This guy sounds creepy as hell if you ask me, like he's watching you."

It was more than a little disturbing, and after the night she'd had on Friday she didn't need anything else keeping her awake.

"Maybe they delivered them to the wrong person."

Carter held up the tiny envelope where her name was neatly typed on the outside.

"These were meant for you. I don't suppose these could be from your ex? Was yesterday any sort of anniversary for the two of you?

Brad? He wasn't exactly the type to send flowers. Far too

practical.

"I can't think of any significance to yesterday," she said, shaking her head. "And I doubt Brad even knows where I am."

"Your family or friends could have told him."

"They know I wanted to make a clean break. They would ask me first." A thought occurred to her. "Maybe the florist mixed up the cards. So the envelope was for me but the card inside got mixed up with another one."

Stroking his chin, Carter nodded. "That's a possibility but it still doesn't explain who sent them. Do you have a birthday coming up?"

Not even close. "My birthday is in July."

Neither of them had any answers and now Mallory didn't want those flowers displayed prominently in her home. She didn't know where they were from but they made her feel slightly icky. A creepy secret admirer sounded stalkerish, not romantic at all.

She picked up the vase. "If these aren't from you I just want to get rid of them."

Carter reached for the heavy flowers. "Tell me where your outside trash can is and I'll toss them."

She kept it in the garage and within seconds Carter had them thrown out while she picked up a few stray petals and leaves that had fallen to the floor. Her fingertip ran along the velvety surface. They'd briefly made her happy but she didn't want to see them anymore. She tossed the scraps into the kitchen trash and stopped to smell the real bouquet Carter brought her the night before that was sitting on her table.

The flowers were out of sight but clearly not out of his mind. "Are there any men at your work that might have sent them?

What about someone in town that's a little too friendly? Maybe the guy that makes your latte or a waiter that brought you extra fries?"

"I can't think of a single person and I'm terrible at flirting. There are a few men at the school where I teach but I don't think any of them are single."

His mouth was a grim, flat line. "Men don't need to be single to pursue a woman, honey. Have any of them shown you a great deal of attention? Maybe gave you compliments?"

"No," she shook her head again, her mind whirring at a hundred miles an hour. Who the hell had sent those flowers? And why? "I swear no one has been weird or creepy. I've got a good sixth sense about stuff like that and no one has tripped it."

Rubbing the back of his neck, Carter finally seemed to accept her answer. "I just want to know who sent them but it doesn't sound like we're going to figure that out easily. But you should be extra-aware from now on. Watch the men in your orbit closely. Whoever sent these will probably want you to acknowledge them."

"I can do that." She hiked her purse higher on her shoulder. "How about we put this out of our minds and go? I can't even think about this when I'm too busy being nervous about eating dinner with your family."

That declaration was rewarded with an easy smile. "Honey, my family already thinks you're aces so you don't have anything to be nervous about. But if you do feel nervous, just pretend they're in their underwear. Isn't that what they always say to do?"

All those handsome Anderson men barely dressed? That would make her blood pressure skyrocket.

Chapter Fourteen

DINNER WITH CARTER'S family had gone well. They were, of course, charmed by Mallory and she seemed to like them too. They'd told some embarrassing as shit stories about him just to see him cringe but she hadn't encouraged it, which was sweet. When he'd told one about his brother Easton they had finally shut up.

Not everyone had attended so she hadn't yet met Travis and Aubrey, who were traveling and Shane and Arden, who had a nasty cold. She did get a chance to meet West, Jason, and Easton's wives and they all seemed to get along well. She'd played with the kids and even held Jason and Brinley's new baby boy Eric, who hadn't spit up or peed on her. Clearly Mallory had the Anderson seal of approval.

Until now Carter hadn't given a shit if his family liked the female he was dating but it was becoming more important as he grew older. Whomever he married would have to deal with the Anderson name, something he'd been doing for over thirty years. Most of the time it was great, but sometimes it could be a burden. He didn't want to throw that on some naive woman who couldn't handle the expectations.

What the hell? I'm not thinking about getting married. I just met this girl.

He liked her, though. More than he had anyone else in recent memory. Thankfully she didn't seem all that anxious to waltz down the aisle, which was a huge relief. She wouldn't be buying bridal magazines after the third date or planning whether to release doves or butterflies at the reception.

He started the car and pulled out onto the long road that would take them to the ranch gate. He really wanted to take her to his house and get cozy in front of the fireplace but he didn't want her to think he was a horn dog that would never take her anywhere and only wanted sex.

"It's still early. Jason's singing tonight at a local bar. He's actually really good. Would you like to go for a little while?"

Carter also wanted to speak with his cousin. When he'd tossed those flowers in the trash, he'd slipped the card and envelope in his pocket. He had a feeling that whomever had sent them was being a jackass after seeing Mallory on the news. Jason might have a few ideas about how to find this guy. Carter wanted to give this jerk a lesson in manners.

Mallory's eyes widened. "He sings? I had no idea. He didn't mention it."

"He's modest—about that, anyway. What do you say? We don't have to stay long. I don't know about you but sitting in front of the fireplace sounds like a great idea later. We're supposed to have record cold tonight."

She nodded with enthusiasm. "I think that sounds like a great idea as long as we're not out too late. I do have to work tomorrow. Is it a karaoke club?"

Carter took the turn toward the highway. "No, he sings with the band. He doesn't do it often but he enjoys it. My aunt has their kids tonight so Jason and Brinley are making an evening out of it."

The drive to the bar didn't take long but finding a parking spot did. The place was packed which was unusual for a Sunday. Word must have leaked out that Jason was singing tonight.

Carter kept his arm around Mallory as they plowed their way through the crowd to a table near the stage. Brinley was there along with Easton and his new wife Dizzy. He'd texted them to save a few chairs.

"Hey," Carter said loudly, holding Mallory's chair for her. "Thanks for saving us a spot."

Easton slapped Carter on the back. "I've had to wrestle at least a half a dozen people for those chairs. It's like everyone in Tremont is here tonight. I didn't realize Jason was this popular."

Carter ordered drinks from the passing waitress before he replied. "That's because you were too busy working to have any fun. Dizzy finally has you living a little."

Dizzy, Brinley, and Mallory were huddled together on the other side of the table deep in conversation like old friends. He was aware that Mallory didn't know too many people in the area, being new. Dizzy was the perfect person for her to get to know. Sweet and friendly, Easton's wife didn't have an enemy in Tremont. She'd have Mallory out and about and maybe even taking art lessons at the community center.

Brinley and Mallory ought to have a few things in common as well since they were both teachers, although the former had taken time off now that she and Jason had a couple of kids.

Easton, despite being a happily married man, gave him a downtrodden expression. "I'm exhausted, man. At my age I need to pace myself. I swear Dizzy's got me doing yoga and now we're working on learning martial arts. She says we need more exercise and less red meat. I miss cheeseburgers a hell of a lot."

Dizzy had some quirky ideas but Carter knew his brother wouldn't have her any other way.

"It could be worse. She could be like her mother."

Dizzy's parents had a habit of doing naked yoga where the neighbors could see them. They liked to celebrate the human body.

"Do you know what she told me at the wedding?" Easton rolled his eyes. "She said if I didn't make her daughter happy she would summon a demon to Tremont."

"And if anyone could do it, it would be her."

"I'm glad they went back to Greece to finish that archeological dig. She kept giving me the evil eye. It was creepy."

Speaking of creepy...

"Listen, don't let Jason slip out of here tonight. I know he and Brinley are anxious to be alone but I need to talk to him."

Easton's gaze sharpened. "What about?"

Carter glanced at the ladies but they were engrossed in their own conversation. With the loud music, it was doubtful they could hear anyway.

"Mallory got flowers on her doorstep this morning. Unsigned card about how great last night was and that the sender couldn't wait to see her again. She thought they were from me but that's not the case."

"And you're jealous? You want to know who sent them?"

For a financial genius, Easton wasn't the best about interpersonal relationships.

"No, I am not jealous. I think that whomever sent these did it to mess with her after seeing her on the news yesterday."

Easton's brows pinched together in concern. "Like a stalker?"

"Maybe." Carter patted his shirt pocket. "I have the name of the florist. I was hoping Jason could nose around and find out who ordered the flowers from them. Then I'll just pay this douchebag a friendly visit. Let him know that it's not nice to be creepy."

"Is she scared?" Easton eyed Mallory and then turned his attention back to Carter. "After what she – and you – have been through it would be normal to be jumpy and nervous."

"Actually, she doesn't seem all that bothered about it but she did have me throw them out, which is when I took the card. She was more nervous about coming to Sunday dinner."

Chuckling, Easton grinned. "We're harmless. Besides, she did great. Mom and Dad love her. They're going to be bugging the hell out of you to keep seeing her."

"I don't plan to stop unless she wants me to."

Carter said it casually enough but the revelation still managed to get a wide-eyed stare from his brother.

"Good call. She's a keeper."

Leave it to Easton to keep the commentary short and sweet. He wasn't much of a talker, not like Noah who could make your eardrums hurt.

"It's still early yet, but I like her."

He could more than like her. Time would tell. But all the indications pointed to Mallory becoming very important in his life.

✦   ✦   ✦

WHEN THE BAND took a break, Carter spirited Jason over to the bar and bought him a beer. His cousin accepted it gratefully but clearly knew it wasn't given out of the goodness of Carter's heart.

"You need to talk to me?"

Carter pulled the florist envelope and card from his shirt pocket, holding it up for Jason's inspection. He accepted it and studied them, finally looking up and shrugging his shoulders.

"And? What am I looking for here?"

Because they didn't have much time, Carter quickly explained the situation to his ex-Fed cousin. If anyone could find out who had sent those flowers it would be Jason.

"And you want me to find him? Then what are you going to do?"

Carter smiled. "Just talk to him. Let him know that sending creepy gifts to women he's seen on television is rude and not nice. I'm not planning on any physical altercation if that's what you're worried about."

Quirking an eyebrow, Jason tucked the card away in his jeans pocket. "But if he threw the first punch, you'd defend yourself?"

"Let's hope it doesn't come to that. So you're going to help me?"

"I will but you may not like what we find. What if it's her ex or maybe an admiring teacher from her school? It might not be someone who saw her on television and then fixated on her."

"Actually, that's exactly what I'm hoping you'll find because it's a hell of a lot less weird. I talked to her earlier and she swears that her ex would never send her flowers like that, and she also says that there are no men at work who stand a little too close and pay a little too much attention to her."

Jason glanced over his shoulder to the table where the women were talking and laughing.

"She might be like Brinley. She has no idea when other men are hitting on her. She just thinks they're being friendly."

Carter couldn't argue with Jason's logic. Mallory was a beautiful woman but she seemed completely unaware of that fact.

"She's had a shitty weekend and I just want to make sure that this guy doesn't make things even worse."

"You haven't exactly had a great couple of days either." Jason leaned in a little closer so that only Carter could hear. "Listen, I know a good therapist that deals with PTSD. If either of you wanted to talk about what happened, she's a good listener."

Jason had been kept as a prisoner by a Mexican drug cartel. Beaten, starved, and tortured, he'd escaped but come home a different man. He had nightmares and often couldn't sleep. A good therapist and settling down with his wife had helped but he would probably always be dealing with his memories of that time.

"Thank you, but I think I'm coping okay. So far. If it changes I'll let you know. I will ask Mallory though, if she'd like the name and number. She's been a rock but it might just be a facade."

"Let me know. When you least expect it to hit you, that's when it comes down like a ton of bricks. Any little thing can set it off. A scent, an image, a sound. Just don't wait as long as I did.

I thought I was too much of a badass to need to talk about it."

Jason drained his beer and then nodded towards the stage. "Don't suppose you want to come up on stage with me tonight? It might impress your girl."

It also might send her running and screaming from the building. Jason was a great singer, Carter was merely okay. All the Andersons could carry a tune but just because they could didn't mean they should. In public, at least. In the shower, Carter was a fucking rock star.

"I usually need a few more drinks in me to do that, but I think I'll let Brinley have the honor tonight. You guys do a great duet."

Jason headed back to the stage, stopping by the table to grab his wife's hand and drag her along with them. Carter stood behind Mallory as his cousin began crooning a soft ballad, Brinley's rich voice mixing in. Placing his hands on her shoulders, he leaned down to whisper in her ear.

"How about a dance?"

She looked up surprised but then smiled and nodded eagerly. That douche of an ex probably didn't ever dance with her either. Carter didn't know this guy and would probably never meet him, but already he didn't like him. Mallory was a catch and the dude had been too stupid to see it.

Their bodies moved together easily, brushing with each beat of the music. Carter pulled Mallory closer, allowing himself the luxury of breathing in her soft, sexy scent. She was a warm bundle of woman in his arms and it was hard to keep his hands in their proper places. If their dancing was any indication of the future, the sex was going to be out of this world fantastic.

Suddenly all he wanted to do was kiss her. And more.

"Honey, how about we head back to your place?"

Her answering smile told him all he needed to know. All systems were go.

Chapter Fifteen

T HE AIR WAS filled with expectation when Carter pulled into Mallory's driveway. She knew what he was thinking because it was what she was thinking about, too. Some force was pushing them together and she didn't want to fight it. He was gorgeous, sexy, funny, successful, and kind. And she wanted him. She was woman enough to admit her desires.

He put the car in park and rounded the vehicle to help her out, his hand strong and warm wrapped around her own. His blue eyes were darker than usual and there was an intensity in his expression that she hadn't seen before. She had a sneaky suspicion that while Carter might be a goof ball out of the bedroom, inside it he'd be all business. At least this first time.

She fumbled with her keys, her hands shaking with her own anticipation. When they were inside they were going to go at each other like animals. Her need had been dammed up too long and he looked like a lion inspecting a gazelle that had wandered away from the pack.

Almost crowing with triumph, she held up the correct key but Carter was already bending down in front of her door, picking up a package.

Uh oh. Not another one. This is not good.

"Looks like your secret admirer stopped by again."

She managed to unlock the door and push it open. So much for passion. Carter's attention was no longer trained on her but that damn box in his hands.

"Just toss it over there. I'll open it later. It doesn't matter."

Clearly it did, though. A muscle jumped in his jaw and his knuckles were white as his fingers tightened on the package. He lifted it to his ear as if he were listening for a bomb.

"I'm sure it's harmless. The flowers weren't dangerous."

"Stand back while I–No, never mind. I'll take it outside and open it. You stay here."

"Seriously?" All the happiness between them had been sucked dry. "You think it's a bomb?"

His lips were a flat line and his blue eyes were an icy gray. "I don't know what it is but I'm not going to take any chances with your safety."

She hadn't known Carter long but arguing with him appeared to be a futile effort.

"Fine, I'll wait here and pour us some wine."

Maybe that would bring the mood back.

He stalked out the front door while she shed her coat, hanging it in the foyer closet. Then she kicked off her shoes and padded into the kitchen. One bottle of wine, two glasses. She could use a drink right about now. She shouldn't because she had to work tomorrow but one little glass wouldn't hurt. It might even help her sleep. She'd had soda at the bar earlier.

She'd barely uncorked the bottle when he came back in, his breath blowing out in a huff of steam before he closed the front door.

"It's candy. Chocolate. And there's a card again."

Pouring two glasses, she met him in the living room, setting their wine on the coffee table.

"What does it say?"

He handed it to her and if anything, he looked more furious than he had a few minutes before.

Sweets for my sweet.

"That's kind of cliché, but it's harmless just like the flowers this morning. I really think it's no big deal."

The look on his face told her in no uncertain terms he thought she was an idiot.

"You think it's just a strange coincidence that this started up right after you're on television?"

Maybe. Sort of.

"Correlation doesn't equal causation."

Isn't that what she said to her students?

He snorted and hopped up from the couch, not touching his wine. "It's a little too much of a coincidence for me, Mal. Some guy saw you on the news and it looks like he's in the early stages of stalking you."

"If I ignore him and don't give him any attention–"

"It might not change a thing," Carter interrupted. "It might make him more determined than ever."

"Or he might go away when he gets no encouragement," she sighed, placing the card on the table. "I'm not saying that this isn't some light stalking. It is weird but I'm not sure what you want me to do here. Lie hidden in wait until he drops off a package and then bash him over the head with a baseball bat? If that's what you want, I can do that. I have a Louisville Slugger in the bedroom that my brother gave me when I moved out of the house and on my own."

Rolling his eyes, he heaved a heavy sigh as if he was greatly put upon to deal with her. Fuck him.

"Don't be overdramatic."

Her? He had nerve.

"I'm not the one thinking that some creepy guy is trying to stalk me. That's all you. Frankly, I think you're the one overreacting. Perhaps what happened at the rest stop has you shaken up more than you want to admit."

Bullseye. If she'd wanted to completely piss him off, she'd succeeded beyond her wildest dreams. His cheeks were red and he was now pacing a hole into her floor.

"Then you're not going to call the police?"

She threw up her hands. "And tell them what? I've had friends who were stalked by men, Carter, and I know how this would go. This person has made no threats against me. They're not going to do anything because they can't. He's broken no laws. Leaving flowers and candy on some woman's doorstep might be in poor taste but it's not illegal."

He stopped and appeared to take a calming breath. "Fine, but I don't want you staying here alone tonight. Come home with me."

Less than half an hour ago she would have welcomed that invitation but now it was coming for all the wrong reasons. Not one had to do with ravishing her naked body.

"I'll be fine," she said in her calmest, most serene tone. They both needed to de-escalate the emotions between them. "He's left a few gifts. He's not going to come into the house in the middle of the night with an ax."

I hope.

He opened his mouth and she braced herself for his arguments but then he snapped it closed. Shoving his hands into his pockets, he pulled out his car keys.

"I'm not going to argue with you. If you think you'll be okay, then I'll just leave you to it. I wanted to help you, but clearly I'm not wanted or needed around here. I wish you good luck."

Before she could even respond, he'd turned on his heel and was stomping out of her house and down the porch. His footsteps echoed in the silence and she fell back onto the cushion of the couch and groaned.

What the hell just happened here? Was this their first fight? And their last? He looked pretty done with her when he'd left. An evening that had begun so promising had just gone to hell in a hand basket.

And she'd be fine. She could handle her own life. She didn't need a man bossing her around and trying to make her decisions for her. He was handsome but he wasn't *that* handsome.

So much for Carter Anderson. She was alone again.

Chapter Sixteen

CARTER WAS ABOUT fifteen minutes down the road when he came to his damn senses. He'd let anger and frustration get the best of him and he didn't always make the best decisions under those conditions. He might be pissed at Mallory – and he was – but he wasn't a total jerk. At least, he didn't think he was.

At the next exit he turned his vehicle around and headed back toward Green Pine, muttering under his breath the whole time. She was stubborn and she didn't listen worth a damn. She seemed to have no understanding of what might be going on.

Mallory was definitely an optimist, serenely going through life so sure it all was going to work out for the best. While it was an attractive trait, it put her in a precarious position, always assuming the best in people and their motivations.

He called bullshit.

He wouldn't label himself a pessimist, but he was definitely a realist. Bad things happened and he'd seen some up close and personal. This asshole hadn't done anything against the law yet but Carter had a nasty feeling about the whole situation. Having cousins who were in law enforcement had educated him early on the signs of *escalation*. If this so-called secret admirer just kept leaving gifts then maybe, just maybe, this was harmless. But if he began to escalate his behavior, then there was no telling what might happen. Obsession had no boundaries and didn't respect the rule of law.

Pulling into Mallory's neighborhood, he kept a close eye out for anything or anyone that would look out of place. It was a quiet Sunday night and the streets were deserted. Most of the homes were dark but there were a few with the lights still on, usually a lone lamp near a window. He was a night owl so he'd be one of them but living on a ranch demanded early rising, no matter how much he'd hated it.

Mallory's home was dark and it appeared that she'd turned in for the night. He parked his car in front of her house and then decided to make a quick trip round the perimeter of her building, just to be sure. It sounded like something West or Jason might do. Carter wasn't a cop and he had little idea as to what he was doing but it seemed like a good idea to make sure there wasn't anyone lurking in the bushes or trying to look into her windows.

If I was a stalker, what would I do?

The structure was a standard townhouse design with three units in each building. Mallory lived on the end so it was easy to go around to the back where the neighborhood butted up against a small city park and a jogging trail. Anyone could easily cut through there to get to her without being seen from the road. While it might look like a selling point to a buyer, security-wise it was rather a nightmare.

Stepping around her folded-up lawn chairs, he knelt down to get a good look into the distance. From here he could see into the park, almost all the way to the children's playground. Mallory needed to plant some shrubbery or tall plants back here to get more privacy.

A blinding light and the sound of footsteps had him whirling around, his heart freezing in his chest. Adrenaline surged through his veins but then he went limp with relief. Mallory was standing there in a pair of flannel pajama pants and a t-shirt, holding a baseball bat over her head.

She did not look amused.

"What in the hell," she hissed as he slowly stood, holding his hands up in defense. The little tornado was still holding that bat in a threatening manner. "My God, you almost gave me a heart attack."

Funny about that... He'd only begun to breathe again seconds ago and his heart was hammering against his ribs as if he'd run a marathon.

"Right back at you," he said, pointing to the bat. "Do you mind? I don't want to get my skull bashed in accidentally. What are you doing out here?"

She looked at the bat and then slowly lowered it to her side. "I heard someone walking around. I wasn't asleep yet. What are *you* doing out here? I thought you'd left."

He straightened his shoulders and cleared his throat. "I did leave and then I came back. And as for what I was doing, I was checking the perimeter, of course."

"The perimeter?" she echoed. "Why? Oh wait, you think an ax murderer might come break into my house."

He didn't want to argue with her again. But damn, she was a stubborn one.

His gaze rested on the bat. "Apparently I'm not the only one who is worried."

In the light of the back patio, he could see the color rush to her cheeks. "Okay, maybe I am a little jumpy, but you're worse."

Sighing, he reached for the bat from her now limp fingers. "I don't want us to fight again. I just want to make sure you're safe."

"And?"

"And I might be more affected by what happened than I originally thought, but let's face it, we both are. This is strange and creepy though. I'm not backing down on that opinion."

Her nose wrinkled but she nodded in agreement. "It is kind of creepy. So I have to ask, just what was your plan in coming back here? Were you going to sleep on my lawn chairs?"

"If you were awake I was going to apologize for stomping out. Since I thought you were asleep, I was planning to check around your house and then go sit in my car."

That seemed to take some of the steam out of her. "All night?"

"I was worried. I have a bad feeling about this. Not that I hope I'm right. I actually want to be wrong. Very, very wrong so you can say *I told you so*."

"I'm sorry, too," she said softly. "I know you were just trying to protect me. It's really sweet that you came back here to check on me even after we argued."

It was nice of me. I'm a nice guy.

He saw her shiver and it was then he realized she wasn't wearing a jacket. Or shoes. She had to be freezing. Her breath was coming out in a puff of steam.

"You need to get inside before you catch pneumonia. It's cold out here. Why didn't you wear a coat?"

She snorted but led the way into the kitchen. "Because I heard someone sneaking around my house in the middle of the night, that's why. I didn't have time for things like shoes and coats." She lifted up the toes on one foot. "I wore socks."

He flipped the deadbolt on her back door and set the baseball bat beside it. "I am sorry I scared you."

"I almost cracked your skull."

She had and he wouldn't forget that lesson. Mallory had a bat and she wasn't afraid to use it. "I have a hard head, at least that's what my family says."

She eyed him, trying to look tough but there was a softness in her gaze. She wasn't mad or angry or anything else. In fact, she might be glad that he came back.

"If you're that worried about me, you can sleep on the couch."

Ouch. Okay, she wasn't super glad. It was better than a cold, uncomfortable car, but not nearly as nice as her warm, soft bed which he might have been in right this moment if they hadn't argued.

If she wouldn't stay at his house, then he'd have to stay here. He might be overreacting based on his heightened emotions from seeing a man die or he might not. Either way, he couldn't walk out when he thought she needed him. If anyone came for Mallory, Carter would be standing in front of her.

She thought he was crazy, and maybe he was.

But she'd walked outside with that bat... She wasn't as confident as she acted. She had her doubts about those gifts, too.

Chapter Seventeen

C ARTER DIDN'T BOTHER to sit in the guest chair in Jason's office, instead perching by the window so he could see outside. He'd been on pins and needles since finding that box of chocolates on Mallory's front porch last night. Hopefully, his resourceful cousin would have the information he needed to settle the question once and for all.

Harmless secret admirer or creepy stalker admirer?

"You're not going to like it," Jason warned, rounding his desk to pull a piece of paper from a drawer. "I wasn't able to find out the identity of who ordered the flowers."

Carter's cousin wasn't a world-class hacker but he had a few who worked for him. If there were bits and bytes with this asshole's fingerprints, Jason and his organization would find them.

"Yet? Or ever?"

Grimacing, Jason lowered himself into his leather chair. "It depends on how you look at it. The order was placed in person and paid for in cash, so there's no credit or bank details to go on."

"Who the fuck pays for an expensive bouquet of flowers in

cash?" Carter asked more so to himself than Jason. "I don't know how much flowers cost but it couldn't be cheap."

Carter rarely carried around more than twenty or thirty bucks in cash. He hardly used it anymore.

"I ordered roses in a vase for Brinley's birthday last month and they set me back a hundred bucks with delivery," Jason replied. "So it is very possible that the person that ordered these was trying to hide their identity. Or it could be that they hate credit cards. I can only give you facts. I can't tell you their motivations."

"So that's it? I just have to give up?"

Leaning forward in his chair, Jason rested his elbows on the desk. "Before I answer that question, you have to answer one of mine. Are you sure about all of this? I'm not saying this is innocent but it could be."

Twisting away from the window, Carter strode over to Jason and looked him in the eye.

"I've got a bad feeling about this, and if you're honest, you'd do the same if it were Brinley."

Jason sat back and smiled. "That's different. Brinley is my wife. Mallory is a lovely woman but you've only had a few dates. Perhaps the trauma of what happened Friday–"

"Knock it off," Carter demanded, waving away whatever lame ass excuse Jason was about to give. "You all are worried about me. I get it. Noah let the cat out of the bag that the family is having secret meetings behind my back since I'm such a fuckup in the romance department. I didn't realize we were so desperate for another wedding in the Anderson family. We just had Dizzy and Easton's not too long ago but apparently that wasn't enough."

"If there are meetings, then I haven't been invited." Jason shook his head. "Jesus, I've never seen a man so torn up about people actually giving a damn about his life. It must be awful to have so many people love you. The horror."

Carter grinned, remembering his cousin when he'd returned from being held hostage by a drug cartel. "You're one to talk. You're worse than me."

Chuckling, Jason admitted defeat. "You've got me there. None of the Anderson men, or women for that matter, are known for how easygoing we are. Well, except for Noah. He's almost comatose. But seriously, I am worried about you. You've been through some shit and you need to deal with it."

"You think I'm avoiding it by making this secret admirer thing a bigger deal than it is?"

"Only you can answer that. Now here's the decision you need to make and you don't have much time to make it. Memories fade and they do it quickly. If you want me to send a man into the flower shop to ask about who ordered the flowers and try and get a description, I will. But—" Jason held up his hand when Carter would have answered. "You need to think about this. Seriously, that's a step in a direction you may not want to go. I need you to be absolutely sure. It was one thing to run a quick transaction, but this is questioning people when this anonymous person hasn't done anything wrong. Creepy? Yes. Illegal? No."

Jason sounded a hell of a lot like Mallory. It might not be against the law to drop off gifts but it certainly wasn't welcome. All Carter wanted to do was make it stop.

"I'll think about it," he finally replied. He was sure about what he wanted but Jason wouldn't be happy unless he thought that Carter was taking his time. "I'll call you later."

"Sounds good. I'm sorry I didn't have better news for you."

Carter turned to leave but paused in the doorway. "I am grateful for your help even if I don't sound it."

"I know you are. You'll know I'm grateful too when you come over next weekend and help me remove that tree stump in my back yard."

"I don't know how Brinley puts up with you. You're a jack-ass."

Jason simply laughed and took a sip of his coffee. "This jack-ass broke about a dozen local, state, and federal laws to get you that information. I do have one more question, though. I haven't seen you this intense in a long time, maybe ever. Is she worth it?"

The answer was out before Carter could even blink. The question was easy. He hadn't known Mallory long but it was as clear as day even to his stupid ass.

"She is."

"Then I'll help you all I can. We all will."

✦ ✦ ✦

THIS WAS A nightmare. A living, breathing nightmare and all Mallory wanted to do was wake up. All day at school people had either stared at her or badgered her with questions about what she'd experienced Friday night. The day had lasted so long she was afraid she was reliving it over and over in some weird parallel universe. Finally, the last bell had rung and she'd gratefully headed out only to find her home had been broken into. The front door was wide open and of course she hadn't had the good sense to stay outside and call the police. Instead she'd walked in when the burglar could have still been pilfering through her belongings. Thankfully he had been long gone.

He might have escaped but it was as if he was still here. That feeling of being violated. Some…person…had come into her home when she wasn't here and clearly rifled through her belongings. There were drawers open, contents strewn about along with books and DVDs scattered on the floor.

Why didn't he just take the television and leave?

Now only three days after dealing with the police at the rest stop she was doing it again, only this time walking around her home with an officer looking for anything that might have been taken.

"I don't see anything missing," she finally said with a sigh of defeat. "Maybe I interrupted them."

What was amazing was that someone was able to break into her home when she had the nosiest neighbor in Montana just across the street. Apparently, Dara had been at the mall near Tremont so she didn't witness any strange happenings. She did, however, find a way to annoy one of the police officers until he asked her point blank if she had anything to add to the investigation. When she admitted that she didn't, he told her to go home until they were done with the crime scene. Mallory had almost cheered out loud.

The young officer had been extremely patient with her, slowly walking through each room to inspect the contents. "It's possible. Did you see or hear anything when you walked into the house? Someone going out the back door perhaps? They could have easily disappeared into that park."

A little factoid that Carter had pointed out to her last night. When she'd purchased her townhouse the park had been a selling point. She would never have neighbors behind her and she could easily hop onto the jogging path for a little exercise. Now she looked at it in a whole new, much more sinister way.

"I didn't hear anything but then I was so shaken up by the front door being wide open."

The policeman gave her a chiding look. "You shouldn't have come in here by yourself. Next time, call us and wait."

"Hopefully, there won't be a next time," she replied shakily, kneeling down on her bedroom floor to stuff her items back into the drawers. She'd sort it all out later. Right now, she simply wanted the room to look like a strange man's hands hadn't rifled through it. In fact, she might just replace it all. There wasn't enough detergent in the world to make her feel better. "So what happens now?"

"We'll fill out a report–"

"Shit," she groaned, interrupting the poor man who was only trying to do his job. "Sorry, I just realized something is missing."

This is bad. So very bad. And icky. Gross and icky.

The officer nodded and shuffled the paperwork on his clipboard. "No problem. We'll note it on the report. If you have the serial numbers we can keep an eye out for the items at the local pawn shops."

Covering her face in her hands, her stomach twisted in her abdomen, threatening to bring up lunch. "I don't have serial numbers for my panties and bras."

His eyes widened and then he swallowed hard, nodding silently. "Oh…yes…I see. Uh, well…I need to be specific on the report. Can you…uh…tell me exactly what you're missing?"

Sure she could and then they could both never make eye contact again.

What has happened to my life? It used to be so boring.

"A matching set of pale blue silk and lace panties and bra. It was a Victoria's Secret set."

The officer cleared his throat, his cheeks bright red. "Size?"

The word came out squeaky and high. This was beyond mortifying.

Blessedly the sound of boots on her wood flooring, saved her from having to answer. Carter stood in the doorway to her bedroom with a fierce expression. His hair was practically standing on end and his teeth were bared in an almost snarl.

"What in the hell?" He stomped forward, barely giving the officer a glance. He rested his hands on her shoulders and pulled her closer so he could look her up and down. "Are you okay? Are you hurt?"

The cop frowned and tried to take control of the situation. "Sir, you are not supposed to be in here. Are you a resident of this house?"

Carter wasn't but she didn't want him to leave. That's why a lie slid smoothly from her lips. Her mother would have been appalled.

"He's my houseguest."

Mallory sucked at lying and by the look on the cop's face she hadn't improved any since the last time. But he didn't contradict her, letting Carter stay in the room and not kicking him literally to the curb.

"I'm fine," she said, addressing Carter. "He was gone when I got home. Looks like he only took two things. At least that I've found so far."

Frowning, Carter glanced around the messy bedroom. "What did he take?"

She closed her eyes and then reluctantly opened them, taking a deep cleansing breath. This was just disgusting.

"My bra and panties."

A look of distaste crossed Carter's face and even the policeman appeared queasy.

"Fuck, that's awful." He wasn't done and she should have known this was coming. "I'd like to talk to whomever is in charge of this investigation. They need to know about Friday night at the rest stop and the gifts you've been getting."

The cop who had been scribbling notes on a piece of paper immediately perked up. Perhaps her case wasn't going to be completely boring after all.

"Friday night? Gifts? Is there more to this, Ms. Cook, that you haven't shared?"

Carter was assuming that all of this was connected. That the murder at the rest stop, her appearance on the news, the gifts, and now the break-in were all intertwined in some way. That simply couldn't be possible. She was having a run of really shitty luck. That's all it was.

Another police officer stuck his head into the bedroom, his gaze darting from Carter, to Mallory, to the young cop, and then back to Mallory.

"Uh, Ms. Cook? Can you come outside, please? You've just received a flower delivery."

Her luck wasn't improving. Carter was going to explode like a volcano.

Chapter Eighteen

AFTER A LONG day on a troubled construction site, Carter hadn't been in the best of moods when he'd pulled up in front of Mallory's house. He was having issues with one of the subcontractors and it might affect the project schedule. If there was one thing Carter hated, it was putting a deadline in jeopardy. It pissed him off, although he usually found ways to avoid it.

But his mood had gone downhill on a sled when he'd seen two police cruisers parked in front of her house, a group of neighbors watching from across the street, and yellow crime scene tape around her front porch.

A million horrifying scenarios had all run through his brain at breakneck speed and every one was scarier than the one before. His heart had lodged in his throat and he'd barely brought the vehicle to a stop before he was jumping out and running into the house, paying no heed to the shouting officers telling him to stop. He wouldn't stop until he saw Mallory safe, sound, and in one piece.

He should never have left her unprotected this morning. It had seemed so calm and normal. He'd fixed the coffee and kissed her goodbye as she climbed into her car, heading off to work. He didn't want to think that was the last time he'd see her alive.

Barely able to breathe, he'd rushed in to the house and found her standing in her bedroom, quite alive and seemingly unhurt. He wanted to see it with his own eyes, though, and hear it from her lips. If anyone had dared to touch one hair on her head, he would hunt them down like dogs.

Then come to find out the perverted bastard had stolen her bra and panties… And now there were more flowers.

This was *escalation* with a capital *E*.

He wasn't overreacting anymore. This wasn't going to go away easily. This asshole was in it for the long haul.

Just as the cop had said, there was another vase of red roses on the porch with a card sticking out of the top. Without pondering the prudence of his actions, he plucked the card from the clip and tore it open.

"Stop right there." Mallory's hand covered his, her tone hard. "You're acting like a bull in a china shop. Let's think this through. If someone really is stalking me, they might want to check that card and envelope for fingerprints or whatever those police labs do. Also, that card isn't addressed to you. It's to me. So hand it over."

Shit, she looked mad. But…

She wiggled her fingers, her brows raised in expectation. Dammit. He handed over the envelope.

Gingerly, holding only the corners, Mallory slid the card out and read it. Her face went pale and her lips pressed together. Whatever it said, she looked like she might throw up. His own belly was churning with anger and bile. This prick needed to be stopped. This wasn't funny or romantic.

She held it out so he could read it.

I wish you had been home when I stopped by. I'll come back an-other time.

Fuck. That was a threat. A boldface threat. She wasn't stay-ing here tonight. Or any other night until they caught this guy.

"You're coming home with me."

He didn't make it sound like a request because it wasn't. If she refused, he'd simply pick her up and haul her very fine ass over to his car and put her in the back seat. He wouldn't leave her here alone. End of story.

He didn't give a shit if he was overreacting after what they'd seen at the rest stop. He didn't care if he was suffering from some sort of trauma and he needed to work through it. She wasn't spending another second under this roof.

When she didn't speak right away, he figured she was think-ing up a reason to stay there which was madness. "I mean it, Mallory. You're not staying here."

The color still hadn't come back into her skin and her hand visibly trembled, holding the card. She was scared whether she wanted to admit it or not.

"I'm not arguing."

There was a first time for everything.

✦ ✦ ✦

MALLORY HAD TO hand it to Carter; when he was determined to do something he did it all the way. He'd somehow managed to help her pack up her belongings while telling the police officer in charge why those flowers weren't a welcome gift. While the cop had been sympathetic it was his opinion and that of his partner that she was being harassed by someone that had seen her on television. Maybe some kids that wanted to scare her.

Why did kids always get blamed for everything? No teenager was dropping a hundred bucks a pop on roses and fine chocolates.

She'd gone immediately numb when she'd read the card. The cold had spread from the tips of her fingers all the way through her veins until she couldn't feel anything, not even the beat of her own heart. It was far easier this way. If she allowed herself to feel the swirling emotions she'd shoved away in her gut, she might lose control. Cry. Scream. Puke. Cry again. Rail against the universe.

This wasn't fair. She'd been in the wrong place at the wrong time. If Carter had driven any slower or faster or if there had been bonus scenes after the movie credits, she might not have been a witness to that poor man's death. She certainly wouldn't be dealing with some crazed stalker and panty thief. In twenty-four short hours this had gone from a slight nuisance to a full-blown threat. She'd barely had time to catch her breath.

Now she was sitting on the guest bed in Carter's house, a place that was becoming more familiar to her with every visit. He'd placed her bag by the closet, inviting her to spread her things out. There was room in the closet and the dresser. The bathroom across the hall was all hers. She'd be staying here for the foreseeable future since her own home had been tainted. She didn't feel safe there anymore and it didn't have anything to do with the flowers and candy. It had everything to do with someone rummaging through her personal items after managing to break the lock on her front door. She'd always thought she was secure behind that lock. She'd been living in a fantasy world.

A big dog. Maybe two big dogs. And a loud alarm with an electrified net. She wasn't sure that even then she'd feel safe.

As if on cue, Tiger entered the bedroom, tail wagging and tongue lolling out. He needed petting apparently and to his credit he wasn't too proud to beg for it. He placed his head on her knee and looked up at her with the most beautiful brown eyes.

Reaching out, she stroked his silky fur and he wriggled closer. "I do feel a lot safer here with you and Carter. Maybe I could take you home with me. Do you think your daddy would miss you? I bet you'd miss him."

She allowed herself the luxury of simply stroking Tiger's fur and cooing sweet things in his ear. It would have calmed her if she was currently allowing herself to feel anything. She could unpack but she didn't have the energy.

With the door open, she could hear Carter speaking to someone on the phone.

"Let's go see what Daddy is doing, okay?"

Tiger's ears perked up and he led the way back into the living room where Carter was finishing up his conversation. He gave her an encouraging smile when she sat on the couch, tucking her legs underneath her. Tiger took of residence on the adjacent cushion.

"I was just talking to Jason. He's headed over here to discuss what we need to do to find out who this person is. I agree that the police aren't going to be able to do much. We'll have to do most of the legwork."

She shrugged and scratched the dog behind his ear. "They don't have much to go on. Thousands of people must have seen the news. He probably paid for these flowers with cash, too. Unless someone recognized him when he ordered them, we have nothing."

Carter came to sit on the arm of the couch, his fingers stroking her soothingly just the same way she was petting the dog. It would be funny if it wasn't her that needed it.

"We have more than you think. There are traffic cameras around your neighborhood that might have seen him come and go."

"He probably came through the park. That's what you said."

Carter nodded. "He might have but even the park has cameras. There are also traffic cameras around the florist shop. If we can find someone who was in both places, that's someone to look at."

That actually didn't sound too bad.

"And if we can't find that?"

"Then we talk to the florist, to your neighbors, anyone and everyone that was around in the last few days. If someone has been watching your house, they've been seen or caught on camera. We can ask – very politely – for any footage from household security cameras, too. Someone might have got him on film."

"If my neighbor Dara didn't see anything, no one did." Letting her head fall back onto the sofa cushion, Mallory groaned. "My brothers told me to put in a security camera but I hadn't gotten around to it yet. If I had, we'd know who it was. I'm so incredibly stupid."

Sliding into the small space between her and the arm of the couch, Carter lifted her onto his lap. He rubbed her spine and pressed a chaste kiss on her cheek.

"Honey, there is no way you could have foreseen this shitstorm. Cut yourself some slack. We'll find this guy."

"In the meantime, you have a roommate. Whether you want me here or not."

That brought a grin to his too handsome face. "Actually, I kind of like having you here. Tiger likes it, too."

The dog seemed to understand Carter's words and scooted closer so she was completely surrounded by grinning male and drooling canine.

She liked it. This was really nice.

I could get used to this. But should I?

Chapter Nineteen

CARTER COULD HARDLY believe his ears. His cousins weren't taking this seriously.

"Do you think I'm overreacting? Because I have to tell you, I'm getting fucking tired of hearing that. This is not a coincidence. Someone is stalking Mallory."

Jason and West exchanged a quick glance and then both of them shook their heads. West held up his hands in a sign of surrender.

"We agree that there's too much going on here for it all to be a coincidence. We also agree that Mallory shouldn't be alone in her home until this is all cleared up. He is clearly escalating and quickly. Almost too quickly."

That captured Carter's attention. "What do you mean...too quickly?"

Mallory entered the living room with a tray of coffee. "I thought you might want this."

Jason smiled and accepted a cup. "Thank you. It does look like it might be a long night."

She turned her attention to West. "I'll echo Carter's question. What do you mean about it being too quick?"

Leaning a hip against the back of the couch, West seemed to struggle to answer. "Of course there are no absolutes but this went from zero to sixty in what feels like seconds. In my experience, stalkers like to toy with their victims. They'd call it courting and dating. They watch for a long time, have casual contact but rarely even address the woman directly. He might get a job delivering pizzas if she orders all the time, or maybe he's the barista where she gets her morning coffee. This contact will often sustain him for a long time."

"Until it doesn't," Jason said, sinking down onto the sofa. "Then the escalation begins. He watches more. Maybe takes pictures. All the while he's fantasizing but his fantasies seem real. He feels like he has a relationship with her, that they're close, maybe even falling in love. All this is happening behind the scenes and the woman might not even be aware that the stalker exists."

"So what's making this one go so fast?"

West scowled and took a sip of the hot coffee. "We don't know. Maybe he's triggered seeing you with Carter."

"My guess," Jason said. "Is that this isn't a stalker at all. This isn't obsession. This is someone messing with you after you were on television. They're enjoying scaring you, watching you react."

Mallory threw up her hands. "Why me? What did I ever do to them?"

"Nothing," Jason said flatly. "Not a damn thing. You simply might resemble someone they don't like or maybe they saw you at the exact wrong time in their life. They're trying to hit out or they're sociopathic and they enjoy controlling people. It could be many reasons but this doesn't feel like a classic stalking situation.

This is someone playing with you for their own entertainment."

"That's sick," Carter said, disgust in his tone. "So what does this mean? That she's not in danger?"

West shook his head. "We don't know that for sure. It's best that she stays here until we can find this guy. Better safe than sorry."

"That sounds great," Mallory replied. "But how are we going to find him and put a stop to this?"

Carter had the answer to her question. "We're already on that, looking at footage and tomorrow morning one of Jason's men will speak with both florists. We'll find him."

They discussed the logistics of keeping Mallory safe for the next few days. They all agreed that she'd be fine when with other people. This guy wasn't going to go after her in public. Not the way he'd been skulking around so far in the shadows.

Mallory went to take a hot bath before bed and Carter walked Jason and West out to their vehicles. The cold air hit him and he shivered, regretting not grabbing his coat on the way. There would be snow soon, any day. He could feel it. Maybe even tomorrow.

"Thanks for coming over. I feel better after talking to you guys. I'm not a cop or Federal agent. I just want to make sure that Mallory is okay."

Jason slapped him on the back. "We weren't trying to bust your balls or anything. We just want to make sure that your thinking stays straight on this. You and Mallory have been through hell and something like that is going to color your thoughts and reactions. Just don't jump to any conclusions. Be cautious, but alert."

West fished his car keys from his pocket. "The Tremont police department has a psychologist that you might want to talk to. Specializes in what you've been through. It might help."

Carter elbowed Jason. "I think I already have the number but thank you. I mentioned it to Mallory and she said she might call and make an appointment."

"And you?" Jason challenged. "You were there, too."

Not quite ready to admit he needed therapy, Carter shrugged. "She said something like it would be nice if we went together. You know, because we experienced it together."

"No shame in talking to someone," West declared, climbing into his truck. "And that poor woman in your home has to be about beside herself. First a man dies in her arms and now some asshole is playing mind games with her. Even if you don't go, don't discourage her from doing it."

"I won't," Carter said as Jason's phone buzzed. His cousin sighed and answered it, checking his watch at the same time. It was late for a call unless it was his wife Brinley.

"Yeah? You're sure? Yes. Okay. I'll call in– Never mind, he's on vacation. Shit, okay. I'll come there myself. Give me twenty minutes."

Jason hung up and shoved the phone back in his pocket. "Duty calls. The firm is getting called in on a local case."

West frowned. "Tremont police? What are they asking you to help with?"

"Not Tremont. Green Pine. They haven't had a murder there in fifteen years so they're requesting our help. They found a body. Man was walking his dog in the park and discovered it. We're shorthanded with Logan out so I'm heading over there myself."

Green Pine? A park? It was a tiny town. How many parks could there be?

"Mallory's townhouse backs up to a park."

West was already shaking his head. "It's just–

"A coincidence," Carter finished for him. He didn't like this development at all. Not one bit. "There are a bunch of them lately. Seriously, could this be related?"

"Remember we talked about jumping to conclusions?" Jason said in a soothing tone he probably used for his baby. Carter wasn't a child but he was worried about Mallory. "I'm sure there is more than one park in Green Pine and even if there wasn't, it doesn't mean that these two incidents are related. But I will check into it, don't worry. In the meantime, I need to get going. They're expecting me at the scene. Go inside and don't say a word about this to her. She doesn't need to be concerned about something that probably isn't even connected to her situation. You'll scare her for no reason."

Carter didn't like not telling her but then he didn't know what he would say. Jason had a point. This might not be related in the least. Every town had crime but that didn't mean that the perpetrator was the same person.

"Call me and let me know."

Jason nodded and climbed into his SUV, giving a wave as he left. West pulled out right behind him, leaving Carter standing out in the cold. Like a fool. Rubbing his frozen arms, he jogged up the steps and into the house.

He'd pretend that nothing was wrong and everything was fine. He only hoped it truly was.

Chapter Twenty

ONE HOT BATH later, Mallory was feeling a little more human. Her life might be a mess but her relationship with Carter wasn't looking too bad. They'd both come a long way from the terrible blind date on Friday night to a place where they trusted each other. If she hadn't believed in his sincerity before, she surely did now after witnessing his discussions with the cops at her home and then his cousins later.

Shrugging on her robe, she slipped a brush quickly through her hair before brushing her teeth. Clean from head to toe, she padded on bare feet out to the kitchen where he was rinsing out their coffee cups.

"Did West and Jason leave?"

"They did. How was your bath?"

"Heavenly," she sighed. "That bathtub is to die for. The whole house is, actually."

The home wasn't large but every inch of it was utilized efficiently. The wood floors gleamed, the stainless steel appliances shone, and the decor looked homey and inviting. Mallory wondered if perhaps his mother had helped with the decorating. He didn't seem the type to pick out drapes and duvet covers but then she hadn't known him that long.

"I built it myself." Carter pressed the start button on the dishwasher and it hummed softly to life. The one in her townhouse sounded like a freight train but she could barely hear his. "I designed it and hand-picked the crew. We all did, although not everyone has a house on the ranch. Some like to live closer to town. Jason bought a fixer-upper and that's how he met his wife Brinley."

Mallory picked up a dishtowel with a cow on it. "Are you really into cows?"

Laughing, Carter plucked it from her hand and tossed it on the other counter. "Easton thought it would be funny to get me those as a housewarming gift with the excuse that they were blue, which is my favorite color. There are all sorts of bizarre things around here from my loving but infantile brothers and cousins. We sort of like to give each other a hard time."

"I noticed that at Sunday dinner. They seem to be particularly hard on you."

So she'd noticed... It probably looked especially bad to an outsider who didn't know that he gave as good as he got.

"I'm the youngest. Don't worry, though. They know full well that if they do something to me, I'm going to do something to them. It's only a matter of time. When they least expect it, that's when they should expect it." Mallory looked a little frightened. "I guess your family doesn't do stuff like this."

"When we were kids we could be cruel but now...not so much. We're all too busy to play pranks on each other."

"I think it has to do with the fact that we live and work so closely together."

"And nothing to do with being competitive as hell?"

Chuckling, he nodded in agreement. "Well, that too. It's in the Anderson DNA. We're always pushing to be better than the others. Easton signed up for one of those obstacle course races a few years back and next thing I know we're all doing it, trying to beat each other's times. It's harmless, really."

She didn't look all that convinced. It sounded kind of shitty when he said it out loud. Like they were pitted against each other by their parents but that wasn't the case at all. If anything, their mother had tried to diffuse the competitions and his father had stayed strictly neutral.

"I think that maybe I'm just not that competitive. I suppose when you put that many males with all that testosterone together they're going to compete with each other."

"All I know is that we've been doing it since I can remember. But we'd never hurt each other or anything. It's all in good fun. Just a friendly rivalry."

Her gaze swept his body and he felt a flush of heat. He liked it when she was bold like that.

"So you don't have any injuries or scars from your…competitions?"

Mallory was smart as a whip. He wasn't going to get one over on her. Ever. But he sure as hell wouldn't mind showing her a few of those scars.

"Now I didn't say that. I spent pretty much every summer in a cast and I think the Andersons had a bulk visit plan for stitches and x-rays, but to be fair many of those were from playing sports. We go all out there, too."

"I'm not surprised," she said dryly. She glanced at the clock on the oven display. "I guess I should be heading to bed. I have work tomorrow and so do you."

He wasn't tired. At least, his mind wasn't. His body was exhausted after a crappy night's sleep on her couch but he wasn't about to tell her that.

"I'm a light sleeper. Just knock on my door if you need anything."

I said hopefully.

"I'm so tired I'll probably fall asleep the minute my head hits the pillow." She almost turned to go but then paused. "Thank you. For everything. I'm not sure what I would have done without you."

"You would have called your family but I'm glad that I'm here and that you didn't have to. Besides, we're in this together, remember?"

She nodded and then stood on her tiptoes to brush her lips softly against his. Far too quick. He wanted more but this was not the moment to ask for it. She'd been through the wringer and she needed her rest.

"Goodnight."

He caught her with one arm, wrapping it tightly around her waist. One more kiss wouldn't hurt. In fact, it might help. He bent his head and captured her lips with his own until they were both breathless and flushed. He was only frustrating himself but it felt too good not to do. He gazed down into her eyes, now all soft and unfocused. Her hair was mussed and her cheeks were pink. Gorgeous.

"Goodnight, honey. Sweet dreams."

He'd be thinking about her.

Chapter Twenty-One

BATHED IN A cold sweat, Mallory awoke with a start, her eyes popping open and a gasp on her lips. She'd been dreaming and it wasn't a sweet one. She was standing in the middle of her home and there were faces in all of the windows watching her. She kept yelling at them to go away but they didn't. When she tried to walk to the door to shoo them gone, her feet were stuck to the floor and she couldn't move. She was frozen like a statue being studied by strangers. Chilling and disturbing.

Leaning back against the pillows, she took several breaths to slow her racing pulse and bring her ragged breathing back to normal. She stared at the ceiling for a long time reminding herself that she was safe here at the Anderson ranch. No one was going to get into this house, especially with Tiger's sensitive hearing. According to Carter, the canine would be barking his head off if even a squirrel ventured near the home.

Mallory glanced at the clock on the bedside table and grimaced. One in the morning and it didn't look like she was going back to sleep anytime soon. The few hours she'd slept had been just enough to keep her from falling back into dreamland easily. If she was going to have nightmares like that, she didn't want to go back to sleep anyway. Being awake was far better.

I wonder if Carter is having bad dreams, too?

No, you think that if you're awake he should be, too.

If they hadn't argued the other night, she might be sharing Carter's bed right now. Then he could have soothed her back to sleep when she woke. But they had argued, and she was lying here in the guest room. Alone. She didn't like it much. The bed was certainly comfortable and the blankets warm. It was a lovely room but she couldn't stop thinking about him sleeping just at the end of the hall. Did he snore? Did he wear pajamas? Did he maybe talk in his sleep? He probably looked really innocent when he slept but she knew that he had a bit of the devil in him.

You could crawl in with him.

She could and Carter might welcome her with open arms. If he was a heavy sleeper, he might not even realize she'd joined him until morning.

Of course, if she were to crawl into bed with Carter she would basically be saying "yes" to sex. The fact that he hadn't even tried to get her to share his bed tonight had left her a little miffed, if she were honest. She hadn't said no because he hadn't asked. If he had, she would have said yes.

He could have changed his mind about them. It was possible, although the way he was acting it didn't seem probable. More likely, he was being a gentleman, which was sweet. And unneeded.

They'd grown close incredibly quickly, far faster than under normal circumstances. If she'd learned anything from watching a man die in her arms it was that life is short and there are no guarantees. If she wanted something, she had to go after it.

I do that all the time.

No, you don't. You sit back and hope things come to you.

It might be time to change.

Did she dare? Would Carter be happy she'd come to him? There was no time like the present to find out. Throwing back the covers, she resolutely climbed out of the guest bed and quietly crept down the hall, patting the head of an alert Tiger who was stretched out on his bed just inside the bedroom door. He'd lifted his head when she'd entered the room but he didn't bark, simply studying her as she crept over to the bed as quietly as possible.

She didn't want to scare anyone. If she was on edge, so was Carter. She didn't need him to throw a punch or bean her with a bat because he thought she was a home intruder.

Man shoots girlfriend in the dark. Film at eleven.

✦ ✦ ✦

CARTER'S ROOM WAS dark except for a shaft of moonlight filtering through a gap in the curtains that illuminated a path to the bed. King-sized and impressive, the bed was a four-poster and lovingly crafted with intricate carvings on each pillar. When she'd toured the house earlier, she'd been especially interested in this room. A man's bedroom said something about his personality.

Carter's bedroom said that he loved comfort, fine craftsmanship, and the color blue.

Lying on his stomach, his muscular back was bare, hinting that he might also be naked under the sheet that covered him from the hips down. As carefully as she could, she climbed onto the mattress next to him, trying not to jar the bed and wake him.

He looked incredibly peaceful and innocent when he slept. His chest rising and falling in an even rhythm, his features in sweet repose as if he didn't have a care in the world. Clearly he wasn't having any trouble sleeping nor did he snore. It would be a shame to wake him. She'd just slide in next to him and curl up on the other side of the bed. He wouldn't even know she was here, but his mere presence calmed her shaken nerves.

Sliding under the covers, Mallory pulled them up to her neck and turned toward the edge of the bed, her back to Carter. It was hours before morning and she needed to find a way to sleep. Counting sheep never worked. What was that thing she'd seen on television? Deep breathing and visualizing? She remembered the breathing part but for the life of her she couldn't remember what she was supposed to be visualizing. Being asleep?

She was awash in his scent, and it clung to the sheets and pillows. Even if he hadn't been lying right next to her she wouldn't be able to stop thinking about him. She could feel his body heat reaching across the few inches of mattress that separated them, warming her chilled skin. Resolutely she closed her eyes and tried to relax her entire body, but she was far too aware of him.

"You okay, babe?"

Mallory didn't know when Carter had woken but she didn't imagine his voice in her head. He'd asked her a question.

"Yes."

The covers rustled as he moved closer, his body spooning hers protectively. Sighing, she relaxed against him. It shouldn't have felt so right – she hadn't known him long – but it did.

"Bad dream?"

She nodded but then realized it was dark and he couldn't necessarily see her clearly. "Yes. I'm sorry I snuck in here and woke you up. I just…didn't want to be alone."

His arms pulled her back against him and he rubbed his cheek against her hair. "It's fine. In fact, it's better than fine. I wasn't sleeping all that great either."

"Liar," she said with a chuckle. "You were sleeping like an innocent baby when I came in here."

That made him laugh and the bed shake. "It's been so long since I've been innocent it's not even a distant memory anymore but it's real sweet that you think so."

"Are you a bad boy, Carter?"

The question popped out of her mouth before she could stop it. Now she was playing with fire.

Getting burned wasn't even a consideration.

"I am," he replied promptly, no hesitation in his answer. "But a bad boy still knows how to take care of a lady."

She almost melted at his words. It had been far too long since anyone had taken care of her in a most intimate way.

"Do you want me to take care of you, babe?"

Yes. A million times yes.

Chapter Twenty-Two

"**E**ASY, BABE. I'LL take care of you."

Carter's low voice was reassuring but Mallory barely heard him, instead solely focused on his work-roughened hands that were gliding under the oversized t-shirt she'd worn to bed. Her last lover's hands had been smooth but Carter's were callused from helping out on the ranch. It was erotic to be caressed like this, the dichotomy of smooth and rough. He made her feel very feminine, which was kind of funny when she thought about it. She'd kind of been a tomboy growing up and her adult years hadn't been much different.

Pulling the cotton fabric over her head, he tossed it aside and then started tugging her panties down her legs. She kicked her feet to get rid of them even faster, her body heating up from his touch. Pushing the covers down, she reached back to hook her arm around his neck and pull him in for a long, slow, and infinitely sweet kiss. Their tongues rubbed together and played a game of tag, which of course Carter won.

He liked playing games but she had a strong feeling he liked winning them even more.

His fingers smoothed down her thighs and then back up,

over her hips and came to rest under her breasts. She shivered and goosebumps broke out over her flesh as his thumbs toyed with her nipples until they pebbled. His mouth found a sensitive spot at the base of her neck, his teeth nipping at the skin and then laving it with his tongue.

Writhing in his arms, she giggled when his fingers tickled her ribs and moaned when those same talented digits plucked at the tips of her breasts, sending arrows of arousal straight to her lower belly. She moved restlessly against him but he had her wrapped firmly in his arms, her back to his front, sheltering her with his own much larger frame. Flames licked at her flesh and swept through her veins. Her head fell back against his shoulder, exposing her neck to his wicked lips and tongue. She'd have marks there tomorrow, a subtle reminder of the carnal evening she'd had with this man.

One of his hands slid down her belly and between her thighs. Her legs spread farther apart of their own accord to give him greater access. There was no point in playing coy. Mallory wanted this and she wanted him. She was already impatient to feel him inside of her but he appeared to be determined to take his time.

A groan escaped her lips when his fingers found her sensitive and swollen pearl. Round and round, his fingers circled the button, sending her arousal into the stratosphere.

So freaking good.

Carter knew his way around a woman's body and at this particular moment she couldn't be more grateful about that. He hadn't been a saint and frankly, she wouldn't want one in her bed. A devil did nicely.

"Come for me, babe," he encouraged, his breath warm and soft in her ear. "You can do it. Come for me and don't hold back."

Mallory didn't intend to. It was as if her body was waking up after a long winter's hibernation. She wanted to roar like a bear striding out of his cave, letting the world know that she was no longer asleep. She'd been on automatic pilot too long. Time to take the wheel.

The coil of arousal that had been building in her belly tightened painfully as his too clever fingers found just the right rhythm to send her over. She tensed for a moment, her nails digging into the flesh of his arm and her eyes fluttering shut.

When her orgasm hit, a disco ball of lights swirled behind her lids and her entire body bowed off of the bed. She cried out with the intensity as waves of pleasure ran through her veins like the creek in the park. Carter held her until she came down from her high, whispering in her ear how beautiful she was and how he wanted to make her do it again.

I am totally on board with that.

Her body was sweaty and shaking when she opened her eyes again. The scent of arousal hung in the air and the temperature in the room had zoomed to tropical levels.

Sitting up, he reached over to the nightstand and rummaged in the top drawer before pulling out a foil square.

"Are you ready for me? Do you want this? Because we can stop here—"

"You better not," Mallory said, shaking her finger at him. "Don't you dare leave me here wanting."

Her vehemence must have tickled his funny bone because he

grinned and laughed. "I'm pretty sure I didn't leave you hanging. In fact, if anything, it would be me that would left that way."

Reaching under the sheet, her hand wrapped around his cock, running her fingers up and down until he wasn't smiling or laughing anymore. He was groaning, his head thrown back with pleasure. Or torture. His entire visage was contorted, so it could have been either. He felt like velvet and steel and she took her time exploring the bounty he offered her, letting her fingernail lightly trace the ridges and veins. She wanted to learn every inch of him.

"Jesus, do you have any idea what you're doing to me?"

His words came out hoarse and deep but he didn't try and stop her. That spoke volumes.

"Well…yes, I do," Mallory giggled. "I'm doing what you did to me. I want to be fair about this."

His head snapped up and the foil square crinkled in his hand. "Fuck fair. I want to be inside of you."

He went up on his knees, ripping open the condom with his teeth and then rolling it on. She tried to help but she was probably more of a hindrance than anything. Together they did finally get it on though and he settled between her thighs, his hands taking his weight.

With his body above hers like this she was reminded of just how much bigger he was. He had such strength but he was so gentle with her at all times. Even now, at this intimate moment he was hesitating, giving her a chance to back out. She wasn't going to.

Running her hands down his chest, they settled on his lean hips, urging him forward.

"Now, Carter. I need you."

He pressed forward, sinking deeply inside of her, her walls stretching to accommodate him. Bending her knees, she wrapped her legs around his waist as he began to move, slowly at first but quickly building speed. She anchored her hands to his shoulders as he thrust in, farther each time until he was in all the way. It felt…amazing.

"Harder," she panted, swaying her hips so that he was rubbing her clit with each stroke. Miraculously, she was building toward another explosion, perhaps even more powerful than the last. "Faster."

With a raspy breath, Carter did just that, his hips snapping forward. "Come with me, babe. I'm getting so close."

Mallory wanted to…she was close as well, but her climax seemed just out of reach. She could almost touch it. But not quite.

As if reading her mind but probably feeling the tension in her body, Carter reached down between them with one hand, his fingers finding her clit. One. Two. Three circles and she was flying off into space. She exploded into little bits of glittering confetti and whirled around the room. At some point, she said Carter's name and squeezed her eyes shut, wanting to blank out the world so she could simply live in this moment.

With one last thrust Carter reached his own peak, a growl of pure male satisfaction ripped from his lips. His head dipped down and he captured her mouth with his own, the kiss ravaging her already overwrought senses. The kiss was a claiming but a promise, too. This wouldn't be their last time together.

Collapsing on top of her, his weight pushed the air from her lungs and she playfully pushed at his shoulders, pretending to cough with oxygen deprivation. He rolled off of her and onto his back, pulling her into his side. To her delight, he couldn't seem to keep his hands to himself. He had to be touching her all the time. He stroked her hair, running his fingers through the strands. He softly caressed every inch of skin he could reach. Every so often, he even pressed his lips to her forehead or her cheek or nibbled at the curve of her shoulder.

I could get used to this.

She could, but should she? So far, Carter Anderson was far more than she'd ever dreamed.

Chapter Twenty-Three

WITH HER LIFE in turmoil, Mallory shouldn't have been in such a great mood but she couldn't keep the smile off of her face the next day. She even caught herself humming a few times, which was a huge sign that something was going on. Normally she made fun of people who hummed all of the time but here she was doing it herself as if she didn't have a care in the world.

Carter had followed her to work this morning and walked her to her room, not taking no for an answer when she'd protested that she'd be fine if he saw her to the front entrance. He was delightfully protective and not in an overbearing male way. Just a sweet and solicitous way that she could get used to.

And the sex was over the moon fantastic. Mallory was gosh darn glad she'd woken him up in the middle of the night and he didn't seem all that upset about it either. They'd both been smiling like idiots over their scrambled eggs and toast this morning.

Even her students seem to have caught on that she was really happy today because she hadn't had one discipline issue all morning. Everyone had their homework, and everyone – okay, most of them – paid attention. If they weren't paying attention at least they weren't disrupting the class. It was more than she could hope for, frankly.

She holed up in her classroom during lunch, munching on some cheese and crackers and reading. It was her one quiet point during the day and she relished it. She should probably start working on grading those exams from her algebra honors class but she was far too jumpy. She'd start in on them tonight.

She was so engrossed in her book she jumped at the sound of knocking at her door. Before she could say "come in," a fellow teacher named Jane stuck her head in.

"I told Lisa at the front desk that I'd bring this to you. I knew you'd be in here eating lunch."

The door swung open and Jane stepped inside carrying a box, all wrapped in red paper with a big gold bow. Mallory's stomach tightened painfully and the food in her mouth turned to sawdust. In any other context a surprise gift would be wonderful but there was no way Carter would have sent her anything with all that was happening. That box was from one person only and she was beginning to get really super pissed about it. He'd forced her from her home and now he'd infiltrated her workplace. A place with kids. Not good.

The only good thing about him dropping off a gift for her at school was that the place had cameras. Hopefully he had been captured on video. They might be one step closer to uncovering his identity.

"You lucky girl," Jane gushed, placing the box on Mallory's desk. "You didn't tell us you had a new boyfriend."

She hadn't, but even if she had this gift didn't have anything to do with him.

"We just started dating," Mallory replied, studying the box as if it was a snake. "I didn't want to jinx it."

"He's a keeper, that's for sure. Don never sends me surprise gifts to work. It's so romantic. What's his name? Is he handsome?"

No, it was creepy. Very creepy.

"Carter, and yes, I think he's handsome."

Jane clasped her hands together and grinned. "So? Are you going to open it?"

"Of course. Let's see what it is."

Reluctantly – oh so reluctantly – Mallory nodded and tugged at the bow. It pulled away easily so she could open the box to reveal a silk scarf in deep scarlet.

Blood red, you mean.

Nestled on top of the silk was a card and Mallory was loath to pick it up and read it. Her heart pounded and sweat pooled at the back of her neck as she lifted it from the box.

This will look beautiful on you.

There was no way in hell she was ever going to wear this scarf. If Carter let her, she would burn it in the gas grill on the patio as soon as she returned home from school today. It was probably evidence though, if this ever went to court or she had to swear out a protective order.

"That's gorgeous," Jane exclaimed, running her fingertips over the smooth silk. "Your man has good taste. Are you going to put it on?"

Oh hell no. Mallory could barely keep her lunch down as it was. If she had to touch it, then all bets were off.

"Not right now. I'll put it on for him later."

Jane gave her an exaggerated wink. "I got it. A private show with…just the scarf. Good for you, Mal. Go get him."

Bile rose in her throat but Mallory managed to swallow it down and somehow not reveal to her friend how creeped out she was.

She shoved the lid back on the box. Out of sight, hopefully out of mind. "I will. Go get him, I mean. Looks like it's almost time for the bell."

Thankfully lunch was over, although Mallory wouldn't have minded the time to have a small nervous breakdown in the girls' room before her next class. Just a little one.

Jane glanced up at the clock on the wall and sighed. "Duty calls. I have twenty-four kids who are going to be conjugating French verbs today. They'll hate me for it. See you later, and congrats on the new boyfriend. I can't wait to meet him. He sounds fabulous."

As quickly as she'd come in Jane breezed out, leaving a cloud of her perfume to mix with the smell of dry erase markers and textbooks. Mallory fell back down into her chair and swung open her large desk drawer. She didn't even want to look at this box for the rest of the day. Not until she had to.

Work first, think about it later. Stowing it in the drawer she closed it firmly, the metal barrier between her and the box making her feel somewhat calmer. If only she could close her brain off from all the thoughts whirling around in it. Compartmentalize her life into neat little boxes. Trauma? Over there. Happiness? Right up front. Creepy stalkers? Way in the back.

If she ignored it would it go away?

✦ ✦ ✦

CARTER GATHERED UP the rolls of blueprints and set them on the conference table in his office. He'd need these in about thirty minutes as West was stopping by to discuss an expansion of Tremont's community center. It had become so popular that they needed more space. Carter had several options for his cousin, one of which included an entirely new location. It was more work but it had the land to accommodate the future growth that West insisted they needed.

"Knock, knock. Can I come in?" Jason stood in the doorway of Carter's office. "Are you busy?"

"I'm always busy but you can come in. I've been waiting to hear from you all damn day. Want some coffee or a soda?"

Jason eased his large frame into one of the high-backed leather conference chairs. "I could go for a soda. It's been a long night and day."

Carter's assistant was super efficient and within a few minutes she'd returned with two ice cold cans. He slid one to Jason, and then sat down at the table. His whole body was on pins and needles waiting to hear from his cousin. So many strange things had happened in the last few days and this new murder might be one more.

"So?"

Jason gulped down half of the can before replying. "Green Pine only has one park, so yes, the body was found behind Mallory's home. I could see the townhouses from the dump site."

That snagged Carter's attention. "Dump site? The murder

was committed elsewhere?"

Jason nodded. "We think so. There wasn't enough blood for the fatal wounds. She was stabbed several times in a frenzy. This dude has anger issues."

"The guy at the rest stop was stabbed."

Rubbing his chin, Jason gave him a grim smile. "Remember how we talked about not going off and making assumptions? We don't know that those two murders are connected. The victimology is quite different on its face. The rest stop appears to be a crime of opportunity but the girl looks like it might have been planned to a certain extent. He had time with his victim."

"How much time?"

"Time enough to strip her of her clothes and then redress her in just her bra and panties. We know that because there wasn't much blood on them, nor were they cut or torn. They would have been if she had been wearing them during the attack."

Carter shuddered at what that poor girl might have gone through before she was killed.

"Torture? Assault?"

Jason drank down the last of the soda. "No sign of torture, which is a blessing for her. She appeared to be in good shape. I don't think he held her too long. There were no extraneous cuts or bruises that we can't explain with struggling against her captor. She fought back so there was skin under her nails. We've sent that to the state lab along with some hairs we found. As for assault, the medical examiner will check for that during the post-mortem. I'm hoping that will come up negative as well."

The psychology of crime had always fascinated Carter. When Jason would tell stories from his days working at the FBI and then the DEA, he would listen with rapt attention. What made a criminal tick? Why did they do it?

"He redressed her?" Carter asked. "Does that mean something?"

"If a killer covers the body it can indicate remorse. I'm not sure a bra and panties can be considered covering the body but he might feel regret afterward. I've seen some crazy shit over the years. We're going to talk to the girl's family and friends. I have reason to believe she was on a date and it might not have been their first one. If we can find out who she went out with then perhaps we can find who did this."

"Why do you think she was on a date?"

"Her lingerie was fancy. I always know when Brinley is planning a romantic evening. She puts away the cotton panties and bras and breaks out the silk and lace. That's what this young woman was wearing so I can only conclude that she had a date as she's not married."

That made sense. It might also make finding the killer a hell of a lot easier, and they could use the break.

"It sounds like you have leads to follow up. That's good, right?"

Jason nodded and levered to his feet, tossing his empty can in the trash. "It is and I better get back to it. I'll keep you in the loop. We're going to run a comparison between the woman's stab wounds and the man at the rest stop. I'm not expecting them to match but with all that's been going on we need to look at every angle. Have you heard from Mallory's stalker since you took her to the ranch?"

"We haven't. He might not even know where she is and

frankly that was the whole point."

Brows raised, Jason chuckled. "That's not how stalkers work, at least not usually. They don't give up too easily. If he doesn't know where she is right now, he'll try to find out, so be on the lookout. He might try and follow her home from work so watch your tail. Be aware of the cars around you and make a mental note of their make, model, and color, especially if you see them more than once."

This super-spy cop stuff was far different than Carter's normal day to day activities but he wouldn't let Mallory down. She was counting on him to keep her safe.

"I will," Carter promised his cousin. "Just let me know when you learn anything."

"Will do. Just keep an eye on your woman. Let us worry about the rest."

Carter wouldn't stop worrying until this asshole was identified and stopped. With Mallory at the ranch, would the man get desperate and show his hand? Eventually he had to slip up, and Carter would be waiting when he did.

Chapter Twenty-Four

A COLD RUSH of air blew through the kitchen raising goose-bumps on Mallory's arm. Despite the chilly temperatures Carter was grilling steaks outside, and he'd just brought them in all covered with aluminum foil and smelling delicious. Her stomach rumbled in approval, reminding her that she hadn't eaten much lunch today thanks to her creepy stalker.

Apparently, Carter grilled almost year-round, which sounded completely batshit nuts but he loved his charred animal flesh. Mallory had delicately questioned whether this was a good idea and then let the subject drop. As long as he didn't expect her to go out there and flip the steaks in the freezing cold she was fine. She was keeping busy making au gratin potatoes and a spinach salad in the warm kitchen.

Like a sane person.

Or rather she was trying to prepare potatoes and salad. God bless Carter, he was trying to teach her to cook. He'd patiently explained what she needed to do in easy to understand instructions. So far she hadn't set the kitchen on fire. It was progress.

"Are they done?"

Carter wore a triumphant smile and it was really cute. Man-adorable cute. He looked like a little boy who had won a trophy the way he was holding that platter of meat. Wow, she was truly smitten. Everything he did was adorable in her eyes. He was even getting her to cook.

"They are juicy, succulent, and just a hair under medium. They're going to be delicious. Wait until you taste my secret blend of herbs and spices. The potatoes should be done as well."

It was a good thing he was keeping track because she didn't have a clue how long they would take to bake. Giggling, she pulled the potatoes from the oven, more cheesy goodness wafting around her nose. She'd done it. With a whole lot of help. They might even be edible.

"Alright Colonel, I can't wait. But I do think that I saw you sprinkling those herbs and spices on the steaks. I may already know what your secret is."

"I brought out a few spices just to throw you off. This blend is proprietary. If you like it and want more, you'll have to stick around so I can make it again."

Was that an invitation? A sly way of asking her to...*be his girlfriend?*

Luckily, he didn't pause for her reply, instead slapping those aromatic steaks on their plates while she fetched the salad and potatoes. Setting the table was her specialty.

They chatted during the meal about their day, Tiger sitting at Carter's feet hoping for a handout. He had told her all about his day but she'd been decidedly closed-mouthed about her gift. The box was stuffed in her school bag full of papers to be graded. She was going to tell him but there hadn't been a good time to do it. She hadn't wanted to ruin dinner.

Dinner's over now.

Any excuse she had was gone and she reluctantly excused herself from the table and retrieved the box with the scarf in it. Carter was going to be furious. Head spinning around on his shoulders kind of pissed off.

Sitting back down, she slid the box toward him. "This was delivered to the school today. And no, before you ask, I didn't see who dropped it off. It went to the office and another teacher brought it to me during lunch. The good news is that there are cameras at the school. If he delivered it himself, he was probably caught on film."

For a man so smart that would be the silliest of errors. He'd been very careful up to this point. But everyone makes mistakes eventually.

Eyeing the box, Carter growled with unhappiness and took off the lid. She'd placed the card back on top of the scarf and he lifted it out, read it, and then tossed it back in.

"I really hate this guy. If he and I ever meet, I'm going to knock out his teeth and break a few ribs. This has gone on long fucking enough."

In reality it had only been a few days but she had to admit it felt like much longer. She, too, was tired of it all and simply wanted her life back. It was weird to walk around and wonder who was watching. A little like being under a microscope, involuntarily. Her sense of privacy and security had been shaken to its core.

Like most people in a modern world she knew deep in the recesses of her mind that privacy in the technical age was hard to come by. Strangers could easily get information about her for a small fee on the internet or, if they had the skills, they could get it themselves. True privacy was a delusion that kept her putting her credit card number into websites when she was shopping. She paid her bills online, shopped online, kept in touch with her family and friends online. Heck, she'd even filed her taxes online for the last few years. And she did it all pretending that nothing bad could ever happen. That she was safe. But the fact was that a determined person could get all of that data and more.

Because how could she function in society if she didn't believe that? Every day human beings put their faith in the system and for the most part the system didn't bite back. It was only in extreme situations like this that technology sucked.

"What are you thinking about?" Carter asked, his brows pulled down. "You're frowning."

So was he but not about the same thing.

"I was just thinking about modern technology. I love it but it hasn't done me any favors here. Pretty much anyone can find out all sorts of personal shit about me all for the low fee of twenty bucks. I was contemplating getting a rotary phone and paying with cash."

From the way Carter was chuckling she'd said something very funny.

"It wouldn't work," he dismissed with a pat to her hand. "I've had multiple conversations with a few of the guys that work with Jason. Real computer guys that can dig into places you wouldn't think anyone can go. I asked about what it would take to live off the information grid so to speak and they explained how to do it, but damn, it's almost impossible. Every waking moment would be taken up with avoiding technology. It sounded exhausting and frankly, a futile effort for the most part."

"That's terrifying," she said solemnly. "Utter horror."

He stood and began to clear the dirty dishes from the table. "I agree but we've built this monster and now we have to live with it. If history is any indication, there will be ten other things that are terrifying in different ways within five years."

He really wasn't an optimist.

"Was that meant to be comforting? Because if it was, you suck at this. Not good at all."

"It was so I guess I need to work on my delivery."

Sighing, she picked up a few of the stray glasses and silverware and followed him into the kitchen. "It wasn't so much the delivery as the content."

"I can't change the content, babe. The truth is the truth."

"Then next time lie to me."

The doorbell pealed and Carter pulled his phone from his pocket, tapping at the screen.

"That's one thing I don't want to do." He smiled and tucked the phone away. "It's Jason. Let's hope he has good news. We'll have to tell him about the cameras at the school."

It was more than Jason. There were two other men with Carter's cousin, although Mallory didn't think they were Andersons. They were handsome but didn't have the same features. All three men had serious expressions which instantly put her on high alert. Her body tensed as they all stood in the living room, her heart beating so loudly she was sure they all could hear.

Will someone just talk already?

Clearing this throat, Jason must have heard her silent plea. "Sorry you haven't heard from me since this morning but this new case has been unfolding rather rapidly. We've been interviewing the victim's friends and family."

There was a long pause as if no one wanted to speak. The tension pulled at Mallory's nerves like a taut bow string that could snap at any moment. She couldn't take it.

"What new case?" she asked, breaking the heavy silence. "Is that why you've brought two friends?"

Jason suddenly appeared to notice that he wasn't alone. Smiling ruefully, he turned to the two other men.

"I apologize. It's been a long day. Mallory, this is Wyatt and Zach. They work for me in my consulting firm and are two of my best men. They're going to be protecting you until this man is caught and arrested."

Her heart stuttered in her chest and her hand flew to her throat in a protective gesture. She didn't need two bodyguards. Did she?

"He hasn't done anything illegal," she replied. "He can't be arrested for sending flowers and gifts."

Jason's jaw was tight and he glanced at Carter before answering her unspoken question.

"He can be arrested for murder. We have reason to believe he killed a young woman and then dumped her body in the park."

Black dots danced in front of Mallory's eyes and her knees turned to water, giving out underneath her. Strong arms caught her before she hit the ground, but she didn't fight with the dark. Instead she gave into it, welcoming the peaceful oblivion even as voices in the distance shouted her name.

Chapter Twenty-Five

"I 'VE NEVER FAINTED in my life," Mallory protested as Carter insisted on slapping cold cloths on her wrists and neck while the three other men looked on in amusement. "That's freezing. Stop it."

"I'm just trying to bring you around."

She pushed his hands away and sat up on the couch, having no earthly idea how she'd ended up there. The last thing she remembered... Shit.

"I'm conscious. Do I look or sound unconscious?"

Somehow she managed to peel the offending wet cloths off of her body and dumped them unceremoniously in a heap on the floor. She'd wanted to throw them at Carter but he'd probably retaliate.

"You sound mad."

"Because you're getting me all wet and cold."

The man named Wyatt cleared his throat and then bent down to pick up the wet cloths before disappearing into the kitchen.

Narrowing her eyes at Carter, she turned her attention to Jason and the man named Zach.

"I'm sorry about that. I think I was just on overload. Less than a week ago a man died in my arms and now you're telling me that you think my stalker is a murderer. My brain simply shut down. Could you be mistaken, I say with hope in my voice?"

Jason grimaced and sat on a chair at the end of the couch while Zach made himself comfortable on the ottoman.

"I wish I was wrong all the time, but I don't think that I am. Maybe you should have a drink while I tell you all that we've learned today."

As suggestions went it sounded like a winner. Carter jogged off to get her a drink and Wyatt returned from the kitchen with two towels. One for the floor and one for her.

I like him already.

Accepting the glass of amber-colored liquid from Carter, she eyed it suspiciously. "What is this?"

"A fine single malt scotch. It should leave a lovely burn all the way down to your belly."

"I've never had scotch in my life. In fact, I mostly just drink wine on occasion."

"Honey," Jason said gently. "This might be a good time to try the harder stuff."

That didn't bode well at all.

Her gaze darted between the men. Carter looked anxious and pale. Jason and his two friends looked sympathetic and worried. None of it made her feel any better. In fact, there was a distinct danger of her dinner coming back up. Her stomach churned dangerously, pushing acid up into her throat. She had to swallow and concentrate so as not to be sick in front of these nice men. It was bad enough that she'd sort of fainted. That was a story she wasn't anxious to share with…anyone. It made her look weak at a time when she wanted to appear strong.

No, she needed *to be* strong.

Carter sat next to her, his arm around her waist. He felt warm, solid, and encouraging which only made her even more tense. What was about to hit her? Could she survive it? Did she have a choice?

"Frankly, Carter Anderson, my life has gone to hell in a hand basket since I started dating you."

She'd hoped it would lighten the terrible tension that had built up in the room and it did. All the men cracked up, their laughter genuine at this shitty moment in time. Carter dropped a kiss on her cheek and his arm tightened slightly, bringing her closer.

"It might not be me," he teased. "Maybe it's you. What was it you said? Correlation doesn't equal causation."

It was hard to argue with her own words.

"It's good that you're keeping a sense of humor about this," Jason said. "That's what will keep you sane in the days to come. Trust me on this."

Carter had told her that Jason had been kept hostage and tortured by a sadistic drug cartel so he did have some wisdom to share. The frightening thing though was that he was equating what he'd gone through for months to her situation. Just how bad was this?

"Thank you. Now can you please tell me what's going on? Why do you suspect my stalker of being a murderer?"

It wasn't Jason who answered but Wyatt. "Our consulting

firm has been asked to help out with the murder of a young woman whose body was dumped in the park behind your house, Mallory. We've been interviewing the young woman's friends and family today. They all had the same story. She'd been receiving gifts from a secret admirer. Flowers, candy, and other things. Same kind of creepy notes."

Mallory's blood ran cold in her veins, her fingertips and lips going numb. "It could be a coincidence."

It didn't even sound like her voice. Instead her words were just an echo in the far distance. Her body was still sitting on the couch but her consciousness had separated from it, hovering just above and simply watching what was happening like a television drama. Right now it was just a story and that poor girl on the couch was someone else. Just a character in this fiction.

The man named Zach shook his head. "Unfortunately, it's not a coincidence. Her home was broken into and some lingerie was stolen. Her body was found wearing that lingerie. Believe me, we wish we had better news. But we're not going to let anything happen to you. If anyone wants to get near you, they're going to have to go through us, and it'll be a cold day in hell when that happens."

Pressing her hand against her chest, Mallory listened for a heartbeat. Yes, it was still beating, which was a shock. She was sure she should have had a coronary episode after hearing what they'd told her.

She was being hunted, played with. By a killer.

This was far worse than some poor man dying in her arms. That was bad enough, but this? How was she supposed to respond? Act? Maybe she should scream and run around. Or faint again. Except that she was wide awake and not even close to passing out. Her body had sucked her consciousness right back in at Zach's declaration and she was no longer separate. She could feel everything. The sound of each breath, not just her own but of the men as well. Her senses were heightened and she could smell and feel the tension and fear wafting off of them. They weren't scared of the killer. No, that would be too easy. They were frightened of how she was going to react.

At the moment, there was only one thing she wanted to do.

"Carter, I think I'm going to be sick."

Chapter Twenty-Six

NOBODY CIRCLED THE wagons like the Anderson family.

After holding Mallory's hair while she'd booted up her dinner, Carter immediately took charge. Rightly shaken and scared, she'd made a few token protests when he'd began making plans with Jason and the others but it didn't take much for her to give in. This was about her security and Carter wasn't about to take any shortcuts.

Within the hour it had been decided that the safest place for Mallory was Dizzy's former house in Tremont. She and Easton had planned to make some upgrades to the home before selling it but Carter had been crazy busy and hadn't had a chance to get a crew out there. Now he was glad because he'd packed up their things to move into the home temporarily and he wouldn't have to worry about a ripped apart kitchen or bathroom.

The house had everything they needed.

Proximity to police and trained medical staff, should the need arise.

Traffic cameras on the roads leading to the house.

No places for a killer to hide like on the ranch. If someone wanted to stalk her, he'd have to do it with lots of people around.

A soon-to-be state of the art security system too. Wyatt had taken charge of that list item and Dizzy's former abode was being fitted with a technological wonder if the claims of Jason were to be believed. A mouse wouldn't be able to get into this house without Carter knowing about it.

Jason must have woken the entire Anderson family as well because Dizzy and Easton were showing Mallory around the house while Carter's parents puttered in the kitchen making casseroles and soup so he and Mallory wouldn't have to worry about cooking. Carter was getting hungry again from the smell of delicious food wafting from the kitchen. Tiger had taken up residence at the feet of Kathy and Peter, hoping he'd get lucky. He would too because Carter's mom was a pushover for the dog and was constantly feeding him.

His brothers, Noah and Shane, were helping Wyatt while Zach talked to Jared on the phone about getting the footage from the school today. Everyone had a job and their only goal was keeping Mallory safe and alive.

Everyone but Carter, that was. He was standing in the middle of Dizzy's eclectic living room and he didn't have a clue as to what he was supposed to be doing. Activity buzzed all around him and he was frozen in place, unsure as to his next step. His instinct was to make himself useful but his heart wanted to be with Mallory.

It hadn't been long but he was really falling for this woman. So strong and invincible. She might have wavered when she'd learned she was a target but she'd stood tall after a few weak moments. Moments she totally deserved. But her innate grit and determination won out and now she was trying to take control of an out of control situation. She was asking Dizzy and Easton good questions and keeping an eye on the men installing cameras and sensors all over the house. She might be scared but she wasn't going to let it beat her.

"She's going to be okay. We're not going to let anything happen to her."

That was Jason, who had paused from his work with Wyatt.

"She's terrified and I can't say that I blame her. Why is this happening? Do you think he saw her on television?"

Jason took a drink of water from the bottle he'd been carrying around. "That's my best guess. We're trying to find out everything we possibly can about this guy. Hopefully we'll have some forensics in the next few days. Jared is working through the night trying to dig up any information as to whether there have been other murders with the same signature, and I've got Zach working on a profile. We'll get him and he won't get within a quarter mile of your woman. He's not expecting this and he's never had to deal with it. There'll be no waltzing into Mallory's life and turning it upside down. That shit is over. Now he's fighting an army and his odds suck."

What Jason said was true. This killer had never come up against anyone with any sort of defense, let alone the fortress they were building around Mallory. He really didn't stand a chance.

"So what do you need me to do? Help Wyatt?"

Jason smiled and shook his head. "You stay glued to Mallory. She needs you and that's the only way you'll feel confident that she's safe. I know what I'd do if it were Brinley."

But Jason and Brinley were husband and wife. Carter and Mallory... They were dating and they liked each other. He wasn't ready to call it love. It was wonderful, though.

"It was Brinley, and you did a decent job of keeping her alive."

A gentle touch on his arm and the smell of vanilla alerted him to the fact that Mallory had joined him along with Dizzy and Easton.

"Did something happen to Brinley, too?"

Jason's nostrils flared at the memory. "Something like that. It turns out that she bought a house right next to mine where a murder had taken place about twenty years ago. Evidence was hidden in the home and the killer wanted it back."

Mallory's eyes widened. "Oh my God, did he get it?"

"No," Jason replied grimly. "We set a little trap for him but I had my men guarding Brinley while we did it. She came through this. Dizzy was fine, and you will be too."

Oh hell. He shouldn't have mentioned Dizzy. Damn.

Mallory's brows elevated as she turned to her new friend. "What happened to you?"

Easton was nervously shifting on his feet but Dizzy simply smiled and linked her arm with her husband's. "The man in the house next door turned out to be a serial killer and I witnessed one of his murders. I called the police but no one believed me because he hid the body in a hard to find crawlspace. But Easton did. He protected me and now that man is behind bars."

"And the house is empty," Carter added. "Because no one wants to live in a house where someone was murdered."

Mallory had turned her amber-colored eyes on him. "I said it was you, and you said it could be me…but dude…it's you. Are you listening to this? The Anderson family must have some kind of curse on it. Everywhere you go murder and mayhem follow. Are there any more stories in your family like this?"

Carter's red cheeks and the embarrassed expressions of his brother and cousin told the truth. Her mouth had fallen open and Dizzy was openly laughing.

"What in the ever-loving hell?" Mallory said, exasperation in her tone. "This is not funny."

"It's kind of funny," Dizzy said, trying to keep a straight face. "The Anderson family isn't cursed but being a part of it means there is always something happening. Never a dull moment but it's totally worth it. We only get the murder and homicide thing every now and then."

"I've gone my whole life without the *murder and homicide* thing," Mallory declared, hands on hips. They now had an audience. Wyatt, Zach, and Shane had joined them. "What else has happened in this family?"

Carter was afraid if he didn't answer that she was going to explode. Her face was a crimson shade and she looked furious.

"We weren't keeping anything from you," he finally said. "None of this is a secret. It's all public knowledge."

"Pretend I don't know any of it."

Jason cleared his throat and was the first to speak. "West's wife Gigi was on the run from her stalker ex-boyfriend, and Travis's wife Aubrey got caught up in a murder in Florida. She was a suspect for awhile but then cleared."

Zach sighed heavily and rolled his eyes. "Leann was a target at her high school reunion. I was her bodyguard."

Shane looked around and shrugged. "What? Arden was never in any danger. Her grandmother is a killer but that's it."

All eyes went to Wyatt, who seemed surprised that anyone was looking at him.

"I'm not even an Anderson," he protested. "What happened to Toni was a complete coincidence. It was that damn haunted house she bought."

Pressing a hand to her forehead, Mallory turned to Noah who had come into the room to see why all the noise had died down. "Are you dating anyone?"

A wrinkle appeared between his brows and he shook his head. "No. Why?"

"Good. Keep it that way. You Anderson men are cursed."

Things weren't looking good for the future of Carter's relationship with this woman.

"I think I missed something," Noah replied slowly, his gaze darting around the room. "What's going on here?"

"Just a little stroll down memory lane," Shane said with a grin. "Don't worry, Mallory. We haven't lost anyone yet and we're not going to start now. You're safe and this guy isn't going to get anywhere near you."

Carter was going to take great pleasure in helping put this asshole behind bars where he belonged.

Chapter Twenty-Seven

MALLORY PULLED THE covers up under her chin while Carter shut off the bedroom light. It wasn't her room or his. It was someone else's and she was here because someone wanted her dead. Just out of the blue. At random. He'd seen her on the television and said, "That one. That's the one I want."

No rhyme or reason. Jason had said that she might be his *type*, whatever that meant. It sounded like she had crappy luck.

"I'm sorry about earlier," she whispered as he settled next to her on the mattress with Tiger zonked out on his huge cushion next to the bed. The house was actually quite lovely, decorated in a colorful and homey style. She'd taken to Dizzy right away, immediately loving the woman's laidback approach to life. Her husband Easton had seemed far more conventional and a little stiff but it was clear they adored one another.

"It's okay." Carter's voice was low as well, although they were the only two people in the house. "I guess I'm just used to all the craziness of my family. The joke is that there's never a dull moment but I have to say that most of the time we are pretty boring. My brothers and cousins have had a rough road to love and happiness but they did get there."

She couldn't stop the next words that came out tumbling from her lips.

"But they loved them. There's a difference."

She didn't expect Carter to laugh and she elbowed him hard in the ribs.

"Oww! Shit, that hurt. I'm not laughing at you, I'm laughing at your assumptions. Trust me when I say that I'm not sure there was always love floating around. Dizzy ordered Easton to get the fuck out of her house when he didn't immediately believe that she'd witnessed a murder. Shane and Arden were at each other's throats for quite awhile after she came back to town. You might say that they eventually loved each other but it wasn't looking good at the beginning."

Rolling onto her side, she pillowed her head on Carter's shoulder. He reached around and tucked her closer so that they fit like two puzzle pieces.

"Can they hear us?" she asked, her gaze roaming the darkened bedroom. They'd installed so much electronics it wouldn't surprise her if the whole place was bugged.

"No. They can't see us, either. The cameras are all outside except for one by the kitchen back door and the other in the foyer. We have complete privacy." His fingers brushed her thigh. "Why? Did you have something in mind?"

Was he kidding? He wanted to fuck in the middle of a crisis?

Except...it wasn't the worst idea in the world. She could already feel herself responding to his body heat and that irresistible scent that only he seemed to have. But still it felt strange. She shouldn't want sex when a killer was hunting her.

"We shouldn't," she heard herself replying, despite the fact that her fingers were tracing patterns on the same ribs she'd just bruised with her elbow. "I mean, it's probably not a good idea. Shouldn't we stay alert or something?"

"We were specifically told to get some rest. Jason has men stationed all around the house and even down the block. No one is going to get within a couple hundred feet of here. We're safe as kittens in their mama's arms."

That was true. She'd been shocked at the number of people that Jason had brought in. Some that worked for him and some were volunteers that worked elsewhere in Anderson Industries or on the ranch. It had been a huge relief and the weight of the world had tumbled off her shoulders. She wasn't in this alone and all of these people were going to make sure she stayed alive.

"How can I want you when I'm supposed to be worried about my life?"

His large hand cupped her jaw and turned her head so her lips were close to his. He brushed them a few times with his own. "It's normal to want to feel alive in dangerous situations. And what makes you feel more alive than making love?"

Carter made sense. But...

"I think you could sell ice to Eskimos," she said. "And convince just about any girl to give up her panties."

She could feel his chuckle under her ear, a deep rumble that sent a tingle down to her toes.

"I'm only trying to convince one. How am I doing?"

"Not bad, but I do think we need to get that rest that Jason mentioned. Somehow I doubt tomorrow is going to be any better than today was."

And I'm really weirded out about all the cameras.

Carter arranged the blankets around them and then pressed a kiss to her forehead.

"Then we'll get some sleep. You're the boss. Please don't worry about things, though. We've got this, babe. Not a hair on your head is going to be damaged. We'll get this guy and you'll be safe."

Keeping her safe and protected here was one thing, but catching this killer was something far different. Far more complex. She couldn't stay here forever behind an armed guard. Eventually…something was going to have to give.

✦　✦　✦

THE SMELL OF coffee was a welcome aroma the next morning when Mallory opened her eyes. The bed next to her was empty but the sheets were still warm. Carter hadn't been up long. He might have gone for a run, though.

Throwing on a robe, she padded on bare feet into the kitchen where her brand new boyfriend was standing in front of the back window that looked over the yard and drinking a cup of coffee. Dressed in a pair of jeans and little else, he looked more delicious than any breakfast. No wonder he was so successful with the ladies.

He must have heard her enter the room because he was all smiles, hugs, and kisses when he turned to greet her. This was a lovely way to wake up in the morning. Two mornings in a row now and she could definitely get used to this. She probably shouldn't; it was still early in their relationship after all, but this was nice.

His arms wrapped around her, strong and warm. "How did

you sleep, babe? Want some coffee?"

"Coffee," she croaked after he dropped another kiss on her lips. Apparently, morning breath didn't faze him in the least. Or morning anything. Normally she didn't like to *engage* until she'd had a shower and brushed her teeth.

Chuckling, he retrieved another mug from the cabinet and filled it with the piping hot elixir that was going to make her feel more human. "You told me to remind you to make sure you had a substitute today."

She'd called last night when she'd realized that she couldn't bring a serial killer into her school. The entire situation was too unpredictable and she wouldn't endanger any more people than she already had. Carter had assured her that if the killer wanted to hurt anyone at her school he could have done it yesterday but she didn't want to take the chance. Especially if he became more desperate to get to her now that she had a half dozen men at any one time protecting her.

"Thank you," she said, checking her phone for the message back from the substitute service. "Looks like I'm all set. I can't stay home forever, though. A few days with a substitute and watching movies instead of working will make the students happy but I can't let us get too behind on our scheduled lessons."

"We'll figure this out as fast as we can."

Carter truly meant it but she wasn't as convinced that this was going to be easy. From what she knew, they had zero clues as to who was doing this.

"I know. It's just going to be a boring day. I assume you all want me to sit in this house all day."

That was going to suck. She wasn't good at doing nothing. Maybe she should call her family and let them know... Nope, that was a bad idea. They'd panic and then all hell would break loose. At least the Andersons were experienced in danger and murder. Strangely, they seemed to take it in stride.

"About that, babe." Carter refilled his own coffee cup. "I don't want to let you out of my sight today. How about you go to Anderson Industries with me? You'll be safe, I promise."

Anything would be better than staring at these walls all day. The home was lovely but it was still a sort of prison. Besides, it would be nice to see what he did for a living. She wanted to know everything about him.

"I'm in. What do I wear?"

Chapter Twenty-Eight

FOR SOME REASON Mallory had pictured the Anderson building as a towering skyscraper, like something out of *Dallas* or *Dynasty*. Maybe it was the way that police officer at the rest stop had said the Anderson name or perhaps it was the way the family seemed to be able to get anything done but she'd carried an image of titans of industry buying and selling entire countries with just a phone call.

It wasn't anything like that.

It was a building, or several buildings actually, enclosing a lovely courtyard with grass, benches, and picnic tables where the employees could eat lunch when the weather was good. The edifice, however, wasn't an imposing structure, instead it was more spread out rather than tall. There was no glass and steel but there was brick.

Wyatt was stationed outside the front entrance and another man whose name she couldn't remember took the back. Zach followed them inside the building but he stayed in the hallway outside of Carter's office, giving them some privacy.

The decor wasn't opulent but it was well-designed, well-decorated, and welcoming. Carter's office was on the third floor overlooking the street. It was large with windows all on one side, a light oak desk near one wall and an oval conference table on the other. Blueprints were tacked up on a white board and about every ten minutes his assistant would walk in with another problem he needed to solve.

Carter needed to clone himself about six times. Mallory sat on a small couch tucked in the corner, curled up with a good book but watched more than read. It was fascinating to see him in action. Not once did he get flustered or overwhelmed. He was constantly in control and his memory was amazing. He seemed to know the smallest details about every project he had going despite the fact that he wasn't onsite every day personally.

After what seemed like the dozenth emergency, his assistant left and Carter finally sat down at his desk to drink his cold coffee. It had been sitting there untouched for the last two hours.

"I think you need a raise. Whatever they're paying you, it isn't enough."

Chuckling, he leaned back in the big leather chair and stretched out his long legs, crossing them one over the other. "I'm the owner's son. Do you honestly think I'm underpaid?"

She nodded toward the door his assistant had just exited. "Judging by the last few hours? Yes. It kind of looks like every-thing is your problem."

"Everything with the construction division is, indeed, my problem. We have several projects going on and while I try and visit all of the sites regularly there is always an issue, whether with weather, permits, crews, or what have you. You know the old saying the buck stops here? Well, it does." He tapped the top of his desk. "If something fails, it's no one's fault but my own."

She studied him for a moment, considering his words. "Carter Anderson, are you a control freak? Because it sounds like it."

"News flash, babe. All of the Andersons are to a certain extent, except maybe Noah. Personally, I just think he's better at hiding it. It's bred into our DNA from birth and nurtured along with a love for the land and a healthy respect for tradition. If you hang around Tremont long enough you'll hear someone say that if you know one Anderson, you know them all."

"It's so much to take on yourself. You could delegate more," she suggested. "I'm sure you have good employees."

"I have the best employees," he stated firmly. "And I do delegate a shit load of work, but there are some decisions that I need to make. My people know their boundaries as we've discussed what they're comfortable taking on and what I'm comfortable giving them. When they're ready to take on more responsibility it's usually me that brings it up first, by the way."

He sounded like a really good manager and someone that would be nice to work for. He came off kind of silly and playful so it was fascinating to see there was another side to him. She should have known it was there though, because of how he'd taken care of things since they'd found out she was in danger.

"You're still a control freak."

"That I am." He sat up in his chair and stretched his arms over his head, yawning. "I think my coffee is ice cold by now. How about a soda? I know I could use the sugar and caffeine."

A cool drink sounded heavenly and she placed her book on the sofa in readiness to offer to fetch the sodas, but Carter was way ahead of her.

"Uh uh, babe. I'll send Tina. I can't have you wandering around this building all by yourself, even if it's only down the hall to the refrigerator. I used to have one in my office but it gave up the ghost a few weeks ago. I need to get another."

Slumping back on the couch in dejection, Mallory sighed. "You can put that on your long to do list or you can delegate it."

He grinned and lifted his laptop off of the desk, holding it out to her. "How about you order one for me?"

She frowned and didn't immediately reach for the computer. "Me? I wouldn't know what to get."

He pointed to a spot on the wall by the table with the coffeemaker. "It used to sit right there. It had a small freezer on the top where I hid popsicles for hot days. That's my only criteria. It needs to fit and I want my popsicles."

He was still holding it out, waiting patiently for her to take it. Why not make herself useful? She wasn't doing anything else except reading, and she had a feeling that Carter was trying to prove that he wasn't as much of a control freak as she thought he was.

She took the laptop from his outstretched hand.

"Fine, but you have to live with whatever I choose."

"I'm okay with that, babe. I'm sure you'll do a great job and I'll love it."

Smooth operator. Charming bastard.

Mallory could fall for a man like this.

Chapter Twenty-Nine

MALLORY HAD THOUGHT she might be stuck in the office all day long but to her surprise Carter packed them both up in his SUV so they could pick up lunch on the way to Jason's office. There was news about the case apparently. Wyatt, Zach, and the other man followed along in their own vehicles but the entire morning had been uneventful. One of Jason's men had even checked her home and there were no new gifts. Her stalker had to know at this point that she wasn't there nor was she at school.

She was surprised by how comfortable she felt in these circumstances. She wasn't shaking in her shoes or crying in the ladies' room.

Confident. She felt *confident* that everything would be okay and that she'd make it out of this situation alive and in one piece. She had a platoon of people watching over her and Carter was almost glued to her side. It was hard to be scared when so many others were putting themselves between a killer and herself. They were right. He'd never come up against something like this. He thought she'd be alone and unprotected, unaware that she was being hunted. This time he'd showed his hand and she knew he was coming. They were prepared.

A quick stop at a local pizza place to pick up lunch and then on to Jason's office, which wasn't part of Anderson Industries. She wanted to ask why he didn't work for the family but was afraid it might be a sensitive question. There didn't appear to be any fallout or tension among the Anderson men but she didn't want to rock the boat.

"How long has Jason had the consulting company?" she asked instead, helping Carter arrange the food in the back seat. It looked enough to feed an army but then she wasn't used to feeding hungry bodyguards.

Carter screwed up his face in thought before answering. "Uh, five years or so? He didn't want to go back to the DEA after he escaped from the cartel but he still wanted to stay in some sort of law enforcement. He also wanted to be able to pick what cases he worked on, although I doubt he says no very often. The business has grown so much he now has another small office in Seattle, lots more consultants, too. Shit, I can't even keep track of them anymore. There was a time I knew everyone by first name."

"DEA sounds so scary. Why did he work for them?"

Carter gave her a strange look. "You don't have a crush on him or anything, do you? Should I be jealous?"

What had she done? This wasn't what she'd intended at all.

"No, not in the least." She shook her head, her cheeks turning pink. "Actually, I was just trying to find a roundabout way to ask why he doesn't work for the family business."

"Ah, but you didn't want to ask so personal a question. Got it. That's not some big secret or anything. Jason was in the military and then went to work as a Fed. He wanted to make a name for himself outside of Anderson Industries. There was never any pressure for us to join the family business. If we wanted to, we were welcome. If we wanted to do something else, that was fine, too. West has never worked for Anderson Industries either. He was in the Army and then was a cop until he was elected mayor. Now he can't get out of the job. He threatens not to run and the town threatens to write his name in. He's done such a good job he's stuck."

"But you wanted to work in the family business."

He grinned, parking the car behind a nondescript two story building just down the street from the pizza place. "I wanted to build things. Anderson Industries seemed like a good place to do that."

Mallory had so many more questions. She wanted to know everything but she was beginning to feel like she was interrogating him. With patience and time, she was sure she'd learned what she wanted to know.

She had to wait to exit the vehicle until Wyatt and Zach were there to escort her into the building, one on each side like a huge concrete wall of protection. For a moment when she was standing out in the open under the bright sunshine, she looked up at the rooftops and windows.

Was there someone up there watching her? It didn't matter, they wouldn't get to her. No one would.

Jason was standing in the doorway of a large conference room, white boards on all of the walls. They dumped the food on the table while Jason quickly chatted with his men. He looked serious. Way too serious. Whatever he had to tell them wasn't good news. Again.

The group dug into the food, filling their plates and settling around the table. Jason sat at the head with Carter on his right. Mallory sat next to Carter while Wyatt, Zach, and West – who had just showed up – sat on the other side. They ate for the most part in silence. West asked Carter about a project they were both working on and then they tried to guess what would be served for Sunday dinner this week.

Ordinary, dull small talk. She had a feeling it was for her, to ease the tension. Maybe Jason was going to tell her they didn't have any clues and she could be in this state of limbo for weeks or months. Or maybe he wanted to use her as bait like on television.

Mallory didn't consider herself brave but she'd probably say yes. She wanted to bring this to an end as quickly as possible and she didn't want this to happen to anyone else either.

When their plates were empty, Jason stood and walked over to one of the white boards on the far wall. He pointed to a photo of a young woman. Dark hair and eyes. Pretty.

"This is Amanda Livingston. Her body was found dressed in her stolen lingerie in the park behind your house, Mallory. She was thirty years old, single, no children. She worked as a barista at a local coffee house. Her friends and family say that she was dabbling in online dating. We're looking into that angle as to how he might have found her."

Then Jason walked to the next white board and pointed to a photo of a man, maybe in his thirties. She knew who he was. She'd seen that photo on the news, although it didn't look anything like what she remembered. His face had been pale and contorted as he'd died.

"This is Matthew Montgomery. He was thirty-two, divorced, with no kids. Like Amanda, he died from multiple stab wounds to his torso. We didn't think we'd find any connection but we asked the forensics lab to see if the wounds matched. It turns out they do. Whatever knife was used on Amanda was used on him."

"That means that the same person did it," Mallory said, her gaze back on the photo of Amanda. There was something about the young woman that kept drawing her back but she couldn't put her finger on what it was. "Will that help you find him?"

"It will, I think. Any connections that we can make help us piece the puzzle together." He paused, his own gaze going to Amanda's picture. "She looks like you."

Mallory swallowed hard, words clogging in her throat. She wanted to deny it but it was right there in living color. That's what had been bugging her. Amanda looked like Mallory.

Her stalker had a type.

Jason walked over to another white board, this one behind Mallory so she had to twist around to see it. "These two women were also killed with the same weapon and found dumped in a deserted area in their own stolen lingerie."

They looked almost exactly like Mallory, too. It was creepy. He hadn't chosen her at random. She'd shown up on television and he'd picked her because of how she looked.

"So what do we do now?" Carter asked, placing his hand over hers. "How does this help us?"

Jason pointed at Matthew Montgomery's photo. "He doesn't fit the pattern. I think if we figure out why he was killed, we can figure out who is doing this and stop him from doing it again."

"And how do we do that?" Mallory asked.

The other men had been quiet this entire time, not saying a word, but West tapped the table with his fingers so they swung their attention to him.

"We reconstruct that night at the rest stop. Second by second. Everything you remember or even think you remember. We need to know why he broke the pattern and we think you may have something in your heads that will tell us."

Chapter Thirty

MALLORY LOOKED A little nauseous and Carter wasn't feeling all that great himself. Reliving that night – again – wasn't an activity he was anxious to do but as West and Jason had explained, it had to be done.

"I have a question," she said. "Do the police know that this murder is connected to three others?"

Jason nodded. "They do now. The three jurisdictions are banding together and have created a task force to streamline the investigation."

"And you're heading it up," Carter guessed. "Am I right?"

His cousin nodded self-consciously. "My consulting firm is. I thought you'd rather speak to me than to one of the other members of the task force."

Carter didn't have time to reply. To his surprise, Mallory stood and walked around the table to a white board located at the far end of the room. Her fingers skipped along its surface and for a moment he wondered what in the hell she was doing but then he saw it.

It was a drawing of the rest area.

Crude and rather lopsided. There wasn't much artistic talent in the Anderson DNA so Jason probably did it. He should have turned the job over to Wyatt or Zach.

She pointed to a rectangle. "The cars were closer than this. He'd parked over the line so there was less than a whole space between us."

Carter remembered now. He'd parked where he had because the now deceased man had parked poorly.

Wyatt smiled. "That's good, Mallory. What else do you remember? Any little thing can be important. No detail is too small."

Standing to join her, Carter studied the bare bones drawing. It was incomplete.

"You're missing the woman that was alone," he said, picking up a marker and drawing a rectangle between his own vehicle and the lone man who had rummaged in his trunk. "She was parked just here."

Zach checked some papers in front of him. "The police drawings had her parked around the side."

"No, she came in right behind us," Carter replied, erasing and redrawing. "I think they have her mixed up with the family that was there. The minivan was sort of parked right at the corner."

"Could you see the parking areas to the side and the back of the building?" Wyatt asked, standing and leaning against the table. "There could have been people parked back there."

Jason was already shaking his head. "We know there weren't. We have the security tapes from the rest stop. Unfortunately, not all of the cameras were functioning and the murder took place in one of those gaps."

"Can we see those tapes?" Mallory asked. "It might remind us of little details we've forgotten."

Or put out of their minds deliberately. Carter had known there was video but he wasn't so sure that Mallory should watch it. She was already having bad dreams, tossing and turning in bed, waking up in a cold sweat. Did she need a movie of her nightmare played out in front of her eyes?

He moved closer to her and bent his head so he was speaking softly in her ear. "Think about that, babe. Seeing it all again. Are you sure you're ready?"

She considered his question for a long minute and then lifted her chin, so determined and strong. He had no doubt she could take on the world if she wanted to.

"I know it won't be pleasant but I think we need to do whatever we can to find this guy."

He couldn't argue with her logic because he agreed. He only wanted to protect her because of how he felt about her.

And how do you feel about her, asshole? Are you in love?

Fuck you. Leave me alone. I might or I might not. I like her. It's enough.

Is it? If she only likes you, is it enough?

Sometimes Carter hated that little voice in his head. He muffled the annoying bastard and put his attention back to the job at hand.

"I agree with Mallory. Let's see the videos and we can fill in the blanks. Hopefully."

He'd hold her hand while they watched.

✦　✦　✦

TECHNOLOGY HAD COME a long way but the video from the rest stop still wasn't high-definition quality. It had been nighttime, of course, and the rest stop was surrounded by trees casting shadows, making it difficult to see clearly. The rest stop was fairly well-lit with lights around the building and in the parking lot, but that only added to the now-you-see-it-now-you-don't atmosphere. One minute a person was easily discernible on video and then next they were shrouded in darkness and shadow.

Or a blank. A few cameras were out of commission and on a list to be repaired. Unfortunately, they had been scheduled for maintenance the week after the murder, which meant there were gaps in the footage. A vehicle or a person would appear and then disappear with no clue as to where they went until they popped up on another camera.

Zach stood by the television and pointed to a car parked by the building. "Okay, here we go. This is where things get interesting. We know from the cameras at the entrance and exit that during the time of the murder it was only you two and the four other vehicles at the rest stop because we counted all the cars that came in for several hours before and they all left as well. What we don't know is if one of those vehicles dropped someone off much earlier to lie in wait."

"I never saw anyone that didn't belong to one of the cars," Mallory said. "Everyone seemed to have a place to be."

Carter nodded in agreement. "I didn't see anyone loitering around. Like Mallory said, they all had a sense of purpose if you know what I mean."

Wyatt nodded. "I do, although if someone were hiding out they wouldn't want you to see them until they were ready to strike. But we think this theory is low down on the list of possibilities. We have other theories that make more sense."

"That someone there did it," Mallory stated. "One of the people in the other cars."

It was the only theory that seemed logical. Except that none of this *was* logical. The man getting killed at the rest stop didn't fit in. Carter wasn't a cop but he'd been around them for the last twenty years or so and the one thing he'd learned was that criminals were stupid. Although some were smarter than others, they all eventually made a mistake. They got sloppy or emotional or they escalated…and that's when they slipped up. This man's murder just might be the mistake they needed.

"That makes it a crime of opportunity, though," West said. "Which doesn't make sense knowing what we know about the killer. He's methodical, patient. He likes to play with his victims. He's not impulsive."

Carter didn't agree. "Everyone is impulsive. They just need the right circumstances. I can be as methodical and rote as the next person but I can also be impulsive as shit. I think the question that we should be asking is what triggered him to kill Montgomery? What set him off? My guess would be fear."

Zach nodded in agreement. "Fear is a powerful motivator and can make a person act out of character. For the most part, our serial probably is very patient and methodical, but if something or someone made him fearful he might act without thinking it through."

Her brows pinched together, Mallory scratched her chin. "You think he's afraid of something?"

Carter's mind was firmly back at that rest stop, his memories in living color. "Just because he's a killer doesn't mean that he doesn't have fear. If I were killing women I would be scared of police, of going to jail, of Mom and Dad finding out."

Jason was smiling. "You would have made a good cop. That's actually an excellent theory, and one to follow up on. So, go on," he urged. "You think he was scared and somehow Montgomery made him feel that. We're just brainstorming here so anything is possible."

Everyone was looking at Carter and it made him uncomfortable. As the youngest in the Anderson clan he wasn't often looked to for advice or counsel. Most of the time, his brothers and cousins were telling him what to do or how to think. This was…new. A little unsettling but not the worst feeling in the world.

The fact was he probably wasn't going to say anything that Jason or West or any of the other guys hadn't thought about at some point.

"Maybe they know each other," Carter finally suggested, his mind ticking away at all the possibilities. "Shit, perhaps Montgomery knew something and the killer had to get rid of him."

"If they knew each other why would the killer do it at a rest stop? Why not do it somewhere private and get rid of the body?" Mallory asked.

"To make it look random," Wyatt replied. "This way he wouldn't be linked to the murder."

Carter stroked his chin. So many possibilities. "He couldn't have known the cameras weren't functioning in the front of the building. He might have been scared and desperate. He didn't put a lot of thought into this."

Jason pointed to the television. "Let's go back to the video. Walk through what you heard or saw. This is you parking your car. You don't get out immediately but when you do Carter checks the tires and Mallory walks around to your side of the vehicle before she heads into the building. What did you see? What did you hear? Was anyone talking?"

Carter let Mallory go first. Her eyes were closed and she, too, was reliving that night in her head.

"It was cold. I remember the chilly air sort of hitting me and waking me up when I stepped out of the car," she began. "Matthew Montgomery's car was to the right of us. He was sitting in the driver's seat and looking at his phone."

The victim's car wasn't visible on the video though. They had to rely on their memories.

"Good, Mallory," Jason praised, pausing the video. "Keep going. What else did you see?"

"The family in the minivan. The kids were asleep in the back seat. The dad was behind the wheel and the mom was with me at the vending machine. She said that she was getting her husband some caffeine because he was tired."

"The dad never got out of the vehicle," Carter said. "He waited with the kids."

"What about the victim?" Jason asked. "Did he get out of his car?"

That night played in front of Carter's eyes, over and over, like a bad Tarantino film.

"No, he didn't. At least not while I was outside. He obviously did when I was in the bathroom."

"What about the others?" Wyatt queried, pointing to the

frozen screen. "What did you see or hear from them?"

Carter and Mallory exchanged a glance, a silent agreement that he would continue speaking. "The woman came in right behind us and the video shows that. She went inside when I did and when I came out of the bathroom she was gone."

Mallory nodded in agreement. "She was gone when I came out of the building as well."

"That leaves one other person," Jason said. "The man that was by himself. Tell me about him."

"I barely noticed him," Mallory replied. "I can't tell you much. Carter?"

Carter had given the lone man a hell of a lot of thought since that night. Mallory had immediately suspected him and that first night he'd defended the guy but... Upon reflection, she might have a point.

"I noticed him. He was rummaging around in the back of his car. It was a hatchback type. I assumed he was rearranging luggage or something like that. He was doing that when we got there and he was still doing it when I went inside the building. He was gone when I came out."

Wyatt's eyes narrowed at Carter's statement. "You have a sort of tone when you describe him. Is there something else?"

Carter didn't have shit and that was the problem. He threw up his hands in frustration.

"No, but he makes the most sense as the killer, doesn't he? The woman probably didn't do it, the family didn't do it. So that only leaves him."

Mallory was frowning and shaking her head. "Why are you giving the woman a pass? Because she's female?"

Carter didn't have time to answer as Zach leaped on the question. "Statistically speaking, he's right. The vast majority of serial killers are men. A woman is rare, although they do exist. But you have a point, too. Our victim was stabbed and that is a woman's method. When they do kill, they like to do it up close and personal."

Charming.

"Okay, what about the family then?" Mallory said, her gaze roaming around the table. "Couldn't the killer be using them as a distraction? Maybe those kids were drugged. Maybe the man and woman work together."

"There have been husbands and wives who have worked together," Zach agreed. "A woman is much more likely to trust a man when he has a female with him."

Jason pushed a button on the remote and the video began to play again. "There's only one problem with all of this conjecture. All of the people at the rest stop had opportunity. They were all alone with the victim while you and Mallory were in the building and then one by one they all left. From what we can find, none of them had motive either. No one. They've been checked out by the police and they're clean, but I think we need to dig deeper. What are we not seeing on this tape? Where does that leave us?"

With nothing. They had nothing.

Chapter Thirty-One

MALLORY HAD A nasty headache and the ibuprofen she'd taken wasn't making a dent. It had been a long day and much more draining than she'd thought it would be, which was actually kind of silly. Of course, it would be difficult to relive a traumatic event. Whatever had made her think it would be a walk in the park? Or at the very least not horrible?

She wandered into the kitchen and opened the freezer, hoping to find something that could be thrown into the microwave. Kathy and Peter had filled it with food but she honestly had no idea what to do with it all. She couldn't, however, expect Carter to do all of the cooking while they were here. She had to pitch in, too. Even if it was inedible.

"I thought I'd find you in here," Carter said, coming up behind her and wrapping his arms around her waist. "I'm fixing dinner, honey. You can do the dishes later. Right now, you have an appointment at the spa."

Twisting her head around, she gave him a suspicious look. "The spa? I don't think so, although I wouldn't mind a full body massage and a facial. Maybe a mani-pedi too."

"Can't help you with most of that but I have run you a nice

hot bath."

Really? Mallory had never had a man run her a bath before. Not once.

"You ran me a bath," she parroted, still not sure he'd said what he said. "Like a for real bath?"

"No, a pretend bath," he teased. "I'm going to strip you down and place you on the bathroom floor. You can play like there's water there and I'll video the whole thing and put it on YouTube."

She narrowed her eyes and elbowed him in the ribs. He was so solid he didn't even flinch. He'd probably barely felt it. "You wouldn't dare."

"I wouldn't," he agreed. "But you have to watch me every minute. I'm known for getting the most creative revenge on my brothers and cousins. You don't want to piss me off, babe."

"I'll take that under advisement."

She kind of admired his nimble mind. Along with a few other more…physical attributes.

Taking her hand, he led her into the master bath where he had, indeed, run a tub full of steamy hot water. The lights were off but there were candles all over casting a golden glow over the room. A stack of towels had been placed on a chair and a glass of red wine sat on the edge of the tub.

The room was warm and humid, the air scented delicately with something floral. Perhaps jasmine? She didn't know if it was the water or the candles but the whole room had taken on an otherworldly feeling. They were the only two people left and this room was their entire universe.

Carter plucked an item from the vanity. "I looked spa baths

up on the internet and they said that women enjoy bath pillows. I don't have one of those. I do have this blowup roll-pillow for my neck that one of my brothers gave me for Christmas one year when I was having back problems. It's not ideal but it's better than nothing."

Mallory had to clear her throat to dislodge the lump that had taken up residence there. He'd gone to so much trouble. Not only had she never had a man run a bath for her, she'd never had one go to such lengths to make it special.

I take back everything I said about him that first night.

Taking the pillow from his hand, she placed it next to the wine glass. "You are so getting lucky, Carter Anderson. Brace yourself."

His face lit up and his smile widened. "What about your bath? The water will get cold."

"We're going to generate enough heat to make the water boil."

✦　✦　✦

THEY NEVER MADE it to the bathtub.

Carter didn't know if he'd been the first one to make a grab for her or if she had grabbed him, but they'd ended up with Mallory sitting bare ass naked on the vanity and him standing between her spread thighs. He kicked away his jeans and boxers while her impatient fingers tugged his t-shirt over his head. She tossed it on the floor where all the rest of their discarded clothing had piled up. They were too busy to care. Damn, but he loved a woman who went after what she wanted. Mallory gave as good as she got, and she wasn't shy about it.

He couldn't touch her enough, his hands running all over her silky soft skin. Cupping her breasts, he played with the nipples, watching them tighten right before his eyes. The fact that he could affect her this way had aroused him as well, his cock standing at full attention. Already aching, ready and eager to sink deep into her tight heat.

Mallory giggled when he tickled a spot at the base of her neck with his tongue so he nipped at the skin until she was writhing in his arms. Her head fell back and she closed her eyes, licking her full lips. Was there any more beautiful sight than this woman laid out bare before him like an X-rated buffet? She was gorgeous and he couldn't believe that there had been a time when he'd thought they didn't have anything in common. They had chemistry to spare and she made him laugh, too.

How lucky could one man get?

Burying his face in her long fragrant tresses, he nudged at her entrance before realizing his memory sucked. He'd shoved condoms in the pocket of his jeans. Just in case she was over-whelmed with lust and gratitude that he'd run her a bath. He just couldn't believe that it had actually worked.

Carter backed away slightly and she whined, her fingers tightening on his arm. "Easy, babe. I need to get some protec-tion. It will only take a minute."

Scrambling to retrieve the foil packet, he heard another gig-gle and turned to find her hand clapped over her mouth trying to keep in the laughter.

"What's so funny?"

She removed her hand but the laughter kept coming until she had tears leaking from her eyes. Bewildered, Carter was starting to get concerned and a little pissed off. They were having a carnal moment here and now she was laughing.

"Care to share what's so damn funny?"

She pointed at him, her face bright red, her shoulders shaking with mirth. "You–you–you mooned me, Carter Anderson."

Inwardly groaning, he slapped his forehead in shame. Christ, he hadn't even been thinking about it. He'd just been in a hurry to grab the condoms.

Way to ruin a mood, Romeo.

"I'm so sorr–"

He never finished his apology because she'd smashed her lips against his. Okay, maybe the mood wasn't as damaged as he'd thought because her hands had wandered down below his waist and were doing naughty things to his cock and balls. She scraped her nails gently over his sac and he almost went down to his knees as the arousal coursed through him, centering on his lower back. There were so many things he wanted to do to her but once again his impatience was winning out.

"Like that?" she asked, an angelic smile on her face. She kept doing it over and over until he finally had to step away or embarrass himself. She took that as an invitation to hop down from the vanity and begin kneeling, but he quickly lifted her back to her feet with his hands under her arms.

"No, babe. One touch of your pretty mouth and I'm going to disgrace myself. I feel like a horny teenager with you. There's so much I want to do to your body but I can't wait to be inside of it."

She nodded knowingly. "I understand. I can't seem to wait either. Is that bad?"

"No, we'll get around to that other stuff eventually. Now get your gorgeous little bottom back on that vanity. Since you're as impatient as I am, let's get this show on the road."

He'd never slapped on a condom that fast but somehow the two of them maneuvered the offending piece of latex on his cock. It had been a team effort. Four hands, twenty fingers, all with one goal.

With one thrust he was in deep and he had to pause to savor the absolute supreme feeling that came over him. Her tight walls hugged him, pulling him in even more. Her nails dug into his shoulders as he drew back almost all the way out before thrusting inside. Again and again he pistoned in and out, never getting enough of her. Her scent, her skin, her sighs and moans. From the sounds she was making he'd found a sweet spot that he simply had to give more attention to.

Lifting her right leg, he draped it over his shoulder while letting her lie farther back in his arms, their gazes locked. The pressure built in his lower back and his balls drew up tight as he rode her hard, rubbing that spot deep inside of her over and over. With every stroke her breasts jiggled and he couldn't help but watch in rapt fascination. Her long, dark hair was damp and clung to skin that was covered in a light sheen of sweat. Her full, pink lips were parted as she panted and groaned his name. There was nothing more arousing than Mallory saying his name. He didn't know why, he just loved it.

When she screamed his name it triggered his own release and he thrust in one last time, his climax ripping through his balls and almost sending him to the floor with its force. He had to lock his knees to keep his legs under him as they both rode the waves of their orgasms, her walls clamping down on his cock. He didn't know how long they sat there on the vanity locked in each other's arms, trying to suck oxygen into their starved lungs. They were wet, sticky, and overheated with dumb smiles pasted on both of their faces.

"I think we both need that bath now," she said, pressing her lips to his damp shoulder. "Want to join me?"

Hell yes. Maybe this time they could do all those things – like foreplay – that they never seemed to have time for.

Chapter Thirty-Two

A FEW DAYS later, Mallory looked like she was going to explode. She hadn't been allowed to go to work and she'd spent her days following Carter around and her evenings in Dizzy's home. She was watched constantly and clearly the stress was taking its toll. He wanted to do something special for her, an activity that would get her out of the house. She was in desperate need of fun and a distraction. Jason's investigation was grinding along and in the meantime she had to be protected.

But that didn't mean she had to stare at the same four walls every day. He'd talked to Jason and made some plans that Carter hoped she'd enjoy.

"What do you think we should have for dinner?" Mallory said when they came home from the office. Her shoulders were slumped and she looked a little sad. Hopefully that would change in the next three minutes. "How about chicken?"

He was teaching her to cook and she was a terrible student. That was fine because there wouldn't be any cooking tonight. He was taking her out. She just didn't know it.

"Actually, we have plans. Slap on some lipstick or whatever you women do to look even more ravishing than you already are, and we'll go."

Stopping in her tracks on the way to the kitchen, she whirled around her eyes narrowed in suspicion. "Can we do that? I mean, Jason probably wants me to stay in the house. It's easier to watch me that way."

"I already talked to Jason about this," Carter assured her. "The guy isn't going to try anything in public. That's not how they think he works. Jason and Brinley are going with us along with Wyatt in another vehicle. So what do you say? Want to go on a double date?"

"Yes," Mallory replied, her hands clasped together in excitement. For the first time today her smile seemed completely genuine. "Where are we going?"

"It's a surprise, honey. No need to dress up. In fact, you might want to wear your pajamas."

She approached him, placing her warm hands on his chest and sliding them up and around his neck. "Carter Anderson, you know I don't wear pajamas."

He did and it was glorious.

"I was being facetious, but seriously you don't have to dress up or anything. This is totally casual, but I think you'll like it."

"And it is Jason approved?"

"He thought it was a great idea. Brinley's been itching to get out of the house as well so Mom and Dad are going to babysit."

For a moment a picture of himself and Mallory with a baby passed through his brain and he almost choked on his own spit. Not once in his life had he ever imagined having a child with any of the women he'd dated. Never. And now he knew why. It was terrifying. Not just the being with one woman thing, that wasn't too scary. The part about being responsible for a tiny human being, however, was enough to scare the hell out of him. How did Jason not worry every single minute of every single day?

"Are you okay?" Mallory asked, placing her hand on his cheek. "You turned really pale there for a minute."

No, I'm not okay. I'm clearly hallucinating.

"I'm fine." He bent his head and brushed her lips with his. "Go freshen up. Jason and Brinley will be here any minute. We'll pick up dinner on the way."

Mallory laughed as she headed down the hall. "So mysterious. You're not going to tell me where we're going?"

"A man has to have his secrets, woman."

The biggest secret might just be how important she was becoming to him.

✦　✦　✦

MALLORY HAD TO give Carter credit. He wasn't the typical kind of guy that she usually dated. That first night she'd thought that was a bad thing but now she was thinking that it was good. Very good.

He'd brought her to the drive-in.

A real, old-fashioned drive-in that people rarely saw outside of old films. Jason and Brinley had picked them up in their roomy minivan and they'd stopped to pick up cheeseburgers, fries, and sodas on the way. They'd even made a pit stop for candy, too. Cocooned in their little world – a blue Honda Odyssey – she felt completely safe from whatever was out there and trying to hurt her. Wyatt, the poor man, had the crappy job of following them in his own vehicle. He looked out of place sitting in his car all alone. He was getting some strange looks but, bless him, he simply smiled as they walked by.

"We should get Wyatt some popcorn," Mallory suggested. "He's getting stared at. At least we should make it look like he's watching the movie."

It was a double feature and from the look on Carter's face when they'd rolled up to the gate he hadn't checked what they were playing. It was a tribute to John Carpenter and they were showing *Halloween* and *The Fog*. Probably not the ideal viewing for a woman who was being stalked by a serial killer but she'd quickly assured him that she was fine with it. Mallory liked horror movies and these two in particular. She didn't feel scared because she was fairly sure she wasn't the long lost little sister of Michael Myers, nor had Tremont been cursed a few hundred years ago.

"He's fine," Carter assured her. "He's got tons of food in that car, including a double cheeseburger with the works and those curly fries he likes so much. As for getting stared at, believe me, Wyatt doesn't give a shit."

Mallory craned her neck to see out of the window. Wyatt did appear to be totally okay sitting by himself watching horror movies, but it still didn't seem right.

"He might get scared all by himself."

She must have inadvertently made a joke because all three of them burst out laughing. Carter cleared his throat and explained their mirth.

"Honey, Wyatt is married to a horror junkie. She owns a haunted hotel and entertainment location. Haunted hayrides. Ghosts and zombies jumping out at you. She also designs spooky shit like masks and those animatronic figures that are used to decorate haunted houses. At this point, I bet he's completely immune. If Jason himself came out of those trees with a machete, Wyatt wouldn't break a sweat."

Wyatt's wife sounded interesting and someone that Mallory wouldn't mind meeting someday. "A haunted hotel sounds really cool. Are there really ghosts?"

"When this is all over, I'll take you there for the weekend and you can find out for yourself," Carter promised. "How does that sound?"

"Deal." She nudged Carter's arm and nodded toward a sedan that was parked a few spots down. "Look at those kids. I remember doing the same thing when I was in school."

One teenage boy was opening the trunk of the car and two males climbed out. They'd snuck in so they wouldn't have to pay.

"Those boys are pretty tall. It had to have been a tight squeeze in that trunk," Mallory laughed and Brinley joined in. "When I was young, the girls always got stuck in the trunk because we were smaller."

"Looks like those boys are alone," Jason chuckled. "Sticking females in the trunk is not a good way to impress your date."

"Should we tell them that?" Brinley teased, popping a fry into her mouth. "Sometimes I miss being a teenager. Everything was so simple then."

Mallory spent most of her days with teenagers. "I wouldn't go back for anything. So much angst. What about you, Carter? Would you be a teenager again?"

He hadn't said a word for too long. His entire body was

tense and his gaze was zeroed in on the kids.

"What's wrong? It was harmless fun. You're not going to tell on them, are you?"

Dragging his attention from the teenagers, he shook his head. "No, I don't care about that. But…they made me think of something. Jason, all those people at the rest stop were cleared. But what if…what if the killer was in the victim's trunk? He could have got in before the rest stop and then fled out into the woods. He wouldn't be seen. He'd only have to go a couple of miles before he got to that little dive bar off of the highway. You know that little hole in the wall place that keeps getting shut down. He could have called an Uber or a taxi from there."

The minivan was completely silent. The trunk. It was a possibility.

Chapter Thirty-Three

T HE REQUEST HAD come out of the blue. Matthew Montgomery's family wanted to meet Mallory and Carter, basically to thank them for being there for their son in his last moments. At first she'd wanted to say no in case they asked about those grisly final seconds but then Carter had said that they probably just wanted some closure.

Jason had urged her to accept their invitation but his motives weren't quite as pure. He wanted their cooperation in speaking about their son and where he might have been before he stopped at that rest stop. Jason and the police had managed to procure Matthew's cell phone and laptop from his parents via a warrant but he hadn't had a chance to talk to them since putting together the new theory.

The theory was that Matt had to have picked up the killer – unbeknownst to him – wherever he'd been before. Jason also wanted to know about Matt's friends and his habits. There was a chance that the killer and Matt knew each other. It was a possibility they couldn't ignore.

The problem was asking those kinds of questions without tipping off the parents that it might not be a stranger-murder. It would only scare them and they didn't want to do that to two innocent people.

Jason parked in front of the Montgomery home, a lovely ranch style house in a nice middle class neighborhood. The whole area looked well-kept and normal. Not the place one would expect the victim of a violent crime to live.

"Are you ready?" Jason asked. "Just ask a lot of questions about Matthew. I'm betting they'll want to talk about him. If they ask you any details about that night, I'll try and steer them in another direction. People often think they want all the details but then when they actually hear them it only makes it worse."

Mallory was going to have to live with Matthew Montgomery's dying eyes for the rest of her life. She didn't want to lay that on his grieving parents, too. They had enough on their plates to deal with.

Smoothing the material of her slacks with her damp palms, she nodded. "I don't think I'm going to get any more ready, so we might as well go in. I'm still not sure this is a good idea."

Slipping his hand into hers, Carter gave it a squeeze. "I'll be right beside you the entire time, babe. If you don't want to say much, you don't have to."

Jason walked beside them to the front door. "I agree. Let Carter do the talking. If you really want to get out of there, just say the word and we'll get you out of there."

She tried to cut the tension with a joke. "What word would that be? Help?"

Jason didn't have a chance to answer as the door swung open and a nervous-looking man stood on the other side. Tall and gray-haired, he wore a somber expression along with the red plaid flannel shirt he had tucked into his blue jeans. This had to be Don Montgomery, Matt's father.

"Mr. Anderson." The older man nodded curtly at Jason. They'd met before, of course, since Jason's firm was heading up the investigation. "We've been expecting you folks. Please come in. Gina is waiting in the living room. She made coffee."

The decor inside the home had been chosen more for comfort than style. Overstuffed chairs and couch, family portraits on the walls, and a calico cat snoozing on the windowsill. Gina Montgomery clearly favored floral patterns and the color yellow.

The older woman was setting a tray on the coffee table and straightened to greet them, her hand outstretched. It struck Mallory at that moment what courage it took for these two people to meet her and Carter. They were walking, talking reminders that their son had been brutally murdered.

Jason made the introductions and they all sat down, Carter next to her on the couch and Jason off by himself, leaning against the mantle. There, but only as a facilitator to this meeting. Mallory's stomach churned with nerves and she silently reminded herself to just sip at the coffee. She didn't want it to come back up later. Or now. Normally Mallory loved the rich java smell but the mere aroma was making her queasy. She hadn't been able to eat breakfast this morning so there was nothing in her abdomen but acid.

Gina's hands were shaking as she poured the steaming brew and Mallory had to quell her urge to take the pot and help. She wasn't sure what the reception to that action would be. Instead she smiled at the older woman and murmured thank you. There were cookies on a plate and they looked homemade but no one seemed to have any appetite.

Don placed his hand on his wife's and began to speak.

"Thank you for coming here today. We simply want to thank you for being there for our boy. I wouldn't want him to die—"

A sob from Gina interrupted Don and he moved his arm so it was wrapped around her shoulders. Tears were falling down her cheeks and she futilely tried to wipe them away. Mallory had a feeling that there would be many tears yet to come. They'd only really begun to grieve.

"Want him to die alone," Don finally finished, his head bent close to his wife's. "We're glad that he had someone there. It means a lot to us."

Tears pricked the back of Mallory's eyes and Carter's hand had a deathtrap on her own. No one could be in this room and stay unaffected by the sheer grief of these two parents.

"We're glad that we could be there," she said softly, her throat closing painfully. "We are so sorry for your loss. I'm sure he was a fine man and a good son."

Gina looked up, her blue eyes watery. "He was. Such a good son. He helped around the house and mowed the lawn. Anything we needed, he did for us. He didn't deserve this."

Carter's gaze was wandering around the room, resting on the family photos on the walls and mantle. "Did your son live with you, Mrs. Montgomery?"

She nodded and sniffled into a tissue her husband had pulled from his shirt pocket. "He did. After the Army, he moved back here temporarily but it turned into a permanent arrangement."

"We're not as young as we used to be," Don said. "It was

helpful to have someone around to do the maintenance and the lawn work. I guess we may have to move now…"

His voice trailed off as Gina began to cry in earnest again. Mallory tried not to squirm uncomfortably but this was turning out to be even more horrible than she'd imagined. Carter seemed to sense her unease and took the lead.

"Is there anything we can do to help, Mr. Montgomery? I'm sure you're busy with the final arrangements but if there's something that needs to be done around the house, I'd be happy to get one of my building crews out here. We'd have it fixed in a jiffy."

Gina dabbed at her red nose. "We know who you are. Even here in Lassiter we've heard of the Andersons."

Once again it was like hanging out with *The Godfather* family. If she hadn't spent time with the Andersons and seen just how harmless they were she wouldn't have believed it.

The words *final arrangements* hung heavy over the conversation. Don glanced quickly at Gina before addressing Carter and Mallory.

"The services are tomorrow morning. We'd be honored if you'd come. There will be a small gathering here at the house afterward. Just some friends and family."

Mallory couldn't think of anything she'd rather do less but she would never be so rude as to say no. She didn't want to give anyone else a chance to ask her about Matthew's last moments but she'd go anyway. This wasn't about her.

"Matthew's friends will be there?" Carter asked, his grip tightening again. She'd forgotten about their secondary mission but luckily he'd kept his head together. "That's wonderful."

Gina gave a half-hearted smile. "Matthew wasn't a huge extravert but he had a few close friends that he met on the job at the bar."

Jason, who had been silent this entire time, straightened abruptly. "Job? We weren't aware that Matthew was working at a bar."

Don's cheeks turned a ruddy shade and he sighed. "We didn't want to tell you. Matt was doing some bartending but he was being paid under the table in cash. I didn't want to get the owner in trouble."

"No trouble at all," Jason said, his jaw tight. "We won't hassle the owner but I would like to speak with his friends and coworkers. What was the name of the place again?"

Don and Gina had never said but they handed over the information without hesitation now that Jason had assured them that no one would be in trouble. From the look on Jason's face, that bar just might be their next stop. This could be an actual lead in the case.

The conversation lagged and mercifully Don brought their meeting to a close.

"I'm sure you folks have a busy day. We're grateful that you stopped by and we hope to see you tomorrow."

Carter and Mallory stood, shaking hands again.

"We'll be there," Carter said, reaching for the tray of coffee paraphernalia. "Can I carry this into the kitchen for you, Mrs. Montgomery? It looks heavy."

The older woman smiled and nodded. "Thank you so much. Such a nice offer."

Gina trailed after Carter, leaving Don, Mallory, and Jason in the living room. Mallory cast a wanting glance at the front door but they had to wait for Carter to come back.

Don stepped forward, looming over her and making her take a step back. She wasn't expecting this. "I was wondering, Miss Cook, if you could tell me… now that Gina is out of the room… Did Matt say anything before he died? Anything at all? Maybe his mother's name? It's just–"

The older man broke off and Mallory could clearly see the tears he'd been holding in the entire visit streaming down his weathered cheeks. Jason moved from his spot by the fireplace but she gave him a brief shake of her head. She could do this. She had to.

"He didn't say much," she replied quietly. "He asked for help and that's what Carter and I tried to give him. I'm sorry that it wasn't enough."

A tear escaped from the corner of her eye and her throat closed up, making it hard to speak. She decided that she'd said enough. She'd spoken the truth and that's all these good people wanted. The truth and the killer found.

Don scrubbed at his cheeks with his knuckles. "No need to apologize, Miss Cook. As we said before we're just glad that you were there. Thank you for answering my question. It's been nagging at me since I got the news but I didn't want to ask in front of my wife. She's already so upset. She may never be the same. Matt was her whole world."

"It's fine." Mallory pushed the words out. Barely. Luckily she didn't have to say any more as Carter and Gina returned.

Jason shook Don Montgomery's hand and said that he'd be in touch if he had any news. They all walked to the door and bid goodbye, the awkwardness still there. Nothing was going to make a meeting like this easy and enjoyable.

When they stepped out into the cold air, Mallory took a deep breath. It was over and she'd survived it. The visions of Matthew Montgomery weren't any worse than before. They weren't any better but this wasn't her closure. This was theirs and she was glad she could do her small part.

They had to find the killer. Not just because he was after her but because these people needed justice. It wouldn't bring their son back, but it was all they could give them now.

Chapter Thirty-Four

THE NIGHTCLUB WASN'T open during the day but the manager, a young man who barely looked old enough to drink, was there and able to answer questions. Carter and Jason went inside but Mallory stayed in the car watched over by Zach. The manager named Ray confirmed that Matt had worked there "under the table" a few nights a week.

"Matt was a good guy," Ray said, unpacking liquor bottles behind the bar. "Customers liked him and he was good with the ones that had had a few too many if you know what I mean. He could get them into a cab before they made trouble and a bouncer had to step in."

"Just a few nights a week?" Jason asked. "From what his parents said, it sounded like he was here more than that."

Ray straightened and wiped his hands on a white bar towel tucked into the waistband of his jeans. "He'd come in on his nights off after he was done with his day job. I kind of got the impression that hanging around his parents' house watching *Everybody Loves Raymond* reruns wasn't his idea of fun."

Carter loved his parents but he wouldn't want to live with them full time either. They'd make each other crazy and he'd gain twenty pounds from his mother's cooking.

"Was he here the night he died?" Jason asked.

Ray's smile fell and he nodded. "He was and I wish he hadn't come in that night. Then he wouldn't have been on the road and stopped at that rest area."

"Did he talk to anyone that night? Did he argue with anyone?" Carter asked. "Anything unusual happen?"

Ray thought about it and then shook his head. "Not really. He sat at the bar and chatted like he always does. He was supposed to meet someone but then he left. As far as I know, they didn't show up. His friend left too, right after him."

Friend? Matt was here with someone?

Jason jumped on the bait. "A friend? Who is this friend?"

"I only know his name is Peter. Don't know his last name but he and Matt are tight. Peter's pretty much here every night that Matt is."

If Peter followed Matt out of the bar, he might have witnessed something that could help then track down the killer. Their theory was that the killer had climbed into Matt's trunk before the rest stop. It could have happened right out in the parking lot.

"We'd like to talk to Peter," Jason said. "Do you think he'll be in tonight?"

"He hasn't been in since that night. I think he only came in because of Matt so I doubt I'll see him again."

Shit. How did they track down a guy named Peter? There were way too many in the area. Another dead end.

They needed to go back to Matt and his whereabouts before the rest stop. Carter exchanged a glance with Jason. They were both thinking the same thing.

"Ray, do you have cameras out in your parking lot?"

✦   ✦   ✦

THE FOOTAGE FROM the parking lot was everything and more than they'd ever dreamed. It moved them one step closer to finding the killer. However, Wyatt had been out talking to the florists and he said he had news they weren't going to like. He didn't want to discuss it on the telephone so they gathered in Jason's conference room at the end of the day to hash it all out. They needed to figure out what their next move would be in light of all they'd learned today. Noah and West had joined Jason, Carter, Mallory, Zach, and Wyatt.

Jason stood at the head of the table and pointed to new photos on the white board.

"Let's review quickly so everyone is up to speed with everything we know and the shitload that we don't. We received the parking lot footage from the bar and it did indeed show a man sneaking into Matt Montgomery's trunk. The vehicle was unlocked and so he was able to pop it open with the lever on the driver's side. He climbed in and waited for Matt to drive off. The open question is whether he knew that Matt was going to go to the rest stop before he went home."

Carter wasn't sure why it mattered but then he wasn't a cop. He simply wanted to know who the man was and then get him behind bars so Mallory could live her life without fear again.

"We took a still photo from the footage back to the bar and the manager was able to confirm that the man hiding in the trunk was Matt's friend Peter. We also gave some still photos to

Wyatt to show the florists so we could confirm that Peter is the stalker."

Wyatt cleared his throat. "And that's where this goes south. I visited every florist that had been identified as being used prior to Matt's murder. Not one of them said that this Peter was the man that ordered the flowers."

"So he had a friend do it for him," Carter said, shrugging. "He didn't want to be seen. It makes sense."

Nodding, Wyatt pulled out his phone and scrolled through it. "I thought the same thing too, so I showed them this photo. They all agreed that this was the man that ordered the flowers. All of them except the florist where Mallory's flowers came from, of course."

It was a photo of Matt Montgomery. Their victim. But he was a *victim*.

"Are you trying to say that Matt Montgomery might have been part of all of this?" Carter asked. "Because he ended up dead, too."

"There's no honor among thieves," Wyatt replied. "If a friend of mine was sending flowers to women that ended up dead and he didn't want to show his face in the florist shop so he asked me to do it, I'd either be suspicious or part of it."

Jason taped up the photo of Peter to the board. "Since Montgomery ended up dead, I think the strongest theory is that he was killed to keep him quiet. He may have figured out what his friend was doing and was going to tell someone, or maybe even call the police."

That made sense and it explained so much. Matt was going to turn his friend in and that made him a target. He might have been heading to tell the cops that very night. Carter turned his attention to the map where Jason had marked the homes of each victim in blue, their body dumpsites in red, the bar in green, and the rest stop in orange.

The rest stop wasn't anywhere close to a path to the cops, assuming that Matt would go to his local police. So if he wasn't going to turn Peter in, where was he going? He wasn't headed home. In fact, he was headed in the opposite direction.

"What are you looking at?" Mallory leaned over and whispered. "You're staring at the board so hard it might burst into flames."

His family and friends had overheard and West, sitting across the table, nodded in agreement. "I have the same question. What do you see?"

He struggled to explain it but he wasn't sure it would make any sense to them.

"Peter hides in Matt's trunk and then kills him at his first opportunity. That speaks of desperation to me. So it's logical to believe that Matt was going to turn Peter in and he had to be stopped. But that's not the direction Matt was going. He wasn't headed to the police station. So where was the threat to Peter that made him do something impulsive and out of character?"

There was quiet as they all studied the map with its little dots that weren't speaking up or even helping all that much. Mallory tilted her head and squinted at the board. She didn't have her glasses.

"The rest stop is on the way to the third victim's house," she said, her chin resting on her hands. "The victim that was found in the park behind my home. Do you think that means anything?"

"It might," West replied slowly. "But we have to open ourselves to other theories about this case."

The oldest brother Noah had been quiet up until this point. "You mean be open to the idea that Matt was a part of this, not an innocent bystander?"

Jason shook his head. "We have no evidence to suggest that."

"Don't we?" Wyatt asked. "Matt bought the flowers for Peter. There are two interpretations of those actions and one of them isn't so innocent."

Carter wasn't following their train of thought. "Help a noncop out here. You're being vague."

Zach sat up in his chair. "What they're saying and yet trying not to say all at the same time is that if Matt was an innocent pawn, he was killed because he knew too much or was going to turn Peter in. However, you're right about him not heading to the police station. There didn't appear to be imminent danger to Peter, although he might not have known that. Mallory noticed that the rest stop is almost halfway in between the bar and the third victim's home. That's important because Matt could have been on his way there."

"To warn her," Mallory said. "So Peter killed him before he could get there."

"It's possible but it would have been smarter to call the cops. We have no record of Matt phoning the police. Also, and I think this is important, we don't think that Peter knew that Matt would go stop at the rest area first," Zach pointed out. "That leaves the very unappetizing theory that perhaps Matt was heading to the victim's house to kill her himself. For all we know, they were working together and taking turns. Hell, that may be why Peter killed him. He wanted to do the victim himself and Matt was in the way."

It was a horrifying thought that Matt wasn't the innocent man that they'd all assumed he was throughout this investigation. Having met the parents, Carter could say without a doubt that the Montgomerys would be devastated if that second theory was true.

"Jared is working on Matt's computer and phone," Jason stated. "So we should have something there very soon. And we need to find out who this Peter is. He can answer all of these questions and more. We can stake out the bar and also question Matt's parents. If they were close friends, they ought to know who he is. Perhaps they knew each other in childhood. With any luck, they exchanged texts. Then we've got him."

Mallory half raised her hand. "Um…if they're such close friends…won't he be at the funeral tomorrow?"

If this Peter thought they were on to him? No. But if he thought he was in the clear, they might just get lucky.

"If he's afraid he won't come," Carter pointed out. "If he thinks he's going to be arrested, he won't go near the funeral."

Zach shook his head. "He'll be there. He won't be able to help himself."

A funeral and a killer. Tomorrow wasn't going to be a great day.

Chapter Thirty-Five

THE FUNERAL SERVICE the next morning for Matthew Montgomery was a somber affair. As in so many small towns, there was a big turnout. Everybody knew each other and when they lost one of their own, they all pulled together to mourn. After the service, Jason, Carter, and Mallory drove to the Montgomery home which was practically bursting at the seams with bodies. So many unfamiliar faces but she only wanted to see one.

Peter.

They had a grainy photograph of him climbing into the trunk of Matt's car that fateful night and not much else to identify him. They didn't even know if his real name was Peter.

"Look at all of that food," Carter said, eyeing the folding tables laden down with casseroles, fried chicken, pistachio salad, potato salad, three-bean salad, and a million different desserts. "Their friends must have been cooking for days. The best party of your life gets thrown when you can't enjoy it."

It was quite the get-together. Lots of people, lots of noise. Everyone trying to speak over everyone else and the din would cover anything that Mallory, Carter, or Jason discussed. They could have screamed that they were there to find a killer and she doubted anyone would have blinked an eye.

"I don't know about that," Jason replied with a grin. "My wedding reception was a pretty decent party. I know you had a good time. Didn't you leave with–"

"Not important," Carter interrupted loudly, his cheeks getting warm much to Mallory's amusement. "We're here on business, not to reminisce."

She had a decent idea that he'd left that reception with one of the single bridesmaids. He'd been a hound dog before she'd met him and she was probably crazy to think he wouldn't stay that way. He was just so darn charming... And earnest... And funny... And darn good in bed...

Rolling her eyes at Carter, she poured three sodas into red plastic cups. "As if I didn't know how Jason was going to finish that sentence. Aren't bridesmaids the only reason single guys even go to weddings?"

The question was purely rhetorical. She didn't expect him to answer and he didn't, pretending to be absorbed in people watching.

She handed a cup to Carter and then Jason, keeping the last one for herself. "So what do we do? Mingle? I'm not sure I'd recognize this Peter-person if I saw him. The video wasn't all that clear."

Jason nodded. "Mingling is a good idea. We need to pay our respects to the family so we might make our way to wherever they are."

Raising his brows, Carter ran his gaze over the crowded dining room and kitchen combination. "Any idea of where they might be?"

"My money is the formal living room," Mallory answered, nodding toward the back of the house. "Let's try there."

Easier said than done. The crush of bodies was so dense simply traveling a few feet was difficult. It took them several minutes and about two dozen "pardon-mes" to reach their destination – an orderly line set up for Don and Gina, who were sitting on the flowered loveseat speaking with their guests one by one.

Mallory had been here less than twenty-four hours ago and it wasn't any less awkward the second time. She didn't know what to say or do. Nothing was going to bring their son back and words seemed so inadequate.

"Just say that you're sorry for their loss."

Startled, she raised her head to look into Carter's eyes. His expression was solemn and serious so he must have really spoken, not the little voice in her head. Jason had his back turned to them, chatting with an elderly couple ahead of them.

"What?"

"Just say that you're sorry for their loss," he repeated. "You did fine yesterday."

"I don't feel very comfortable at funerals," she confessed softly, although it was so loud she doubted anyone would hear. Or care what she had to say. "I haven't been to many of them."

"I think it's more about being here than saying the right words. I haven't been to what you might describe as *a lot* of these situations but I think that's what I observed. It was about surrounding the grieving family with people who care."

"I don't know them." Apparently her mouth had a mind of

its own today. "It was a quirk of fate that brought me – us – into their path."

"They're sad. Seeing you, and me too, gives them some sort of comfort. It brings their son closer."

An image of that night ran through her head and she shivered involuntarily. "Or it reminds them of what happened."

"We were invited here," Carter reminded her. "Specifically by them. Whatever it is that they feel when they see us, it seems that's an emotion they want to feel. Now tomorrow or next week it might be different, but for now they seem to want us here. And no, I don't like funerals any more than you do."

This man never ceased to surprise her.

"You seem to know a great deal about the psychology of mourning."

Smiling, he leaned closer. "You mean for a builder, right? I took some psychology courses in college and I thought it was fascinating. I thought about majoring in it but I ended up in architectural engineering."

He was a heck of a lot more than a builder.

"Those two subjects don't have anything in common."

"What can I say? I'm a complex man."

"I'm beginning to realize that."

Jason finished up his conversation with the couple and turned back to Carter and Mallory, a wide smile on his face.

"He's here. My new friends pointed him out. Look right over my shoulder. Short dark hair. Medium stature but thin with a pale complexion. Blue suit that sort of hangs off of him. He was one of the pallbearers. See him?"

Mallory did but…him?

"He doesn't look like a serial killer."

"They never do," Jason replied. "Now after we speak to the Montgomerys I want Mallory to work her way over to the far wall where they put all the flowers. We'll be just a few feet away so don't worry about anything. I want to see if he approaches you."

Mallory opened her mouth to say yes but Carter was already answering for her.

"Hell, no. She's not acting as bait."

"This isn't bait." Jason shook his head, placing his hand on his cousin's shoulder. "We'll never be more than a few feet away. Wyatt is posted at the front door and Zach at the back. We're not going to take our eyes off of Mallory. Remember, this guy doesn't even know we suspect him. He thinks he's in the clear. But if Zach's profile is correct, he's a sneaky and cocky little shit. Let's see if he'll step out of the shadows. That's all we're asking for here. It's up to Mallory. You don't have to if you don't want to."

"I want to," she replied quickly, not wanting Carter to interrupt again. "We need to put a stop to this before someone else gets killed. I feel safe with everyone around. He won't do anything with all these people watching."

"We hope," Carter said grimly. "I can't stop you, but I don't like it."

"That's right. You can't stop me."

Although it looked like he was prepared to physically pick her up and carry her out of the house. Carter was handsome and sexy and funny but he didn't get to order her around. He liked having his way far too much and appeared to be used to getting it. That shit had to stop.

Jason leaned down to speak to her, his voice low. "Stand by that big wreath of red roses. We'll be over by the lilies, not even three feet away. Whatever you do, don't go anywhere with him. If he starts to get weird, just hold your glass out to the right. We'll swarm in. Just see what he has to say. He might reveal himself as your secret admirer. Just don't let him know that we have any idea who he is."

"And then what?" Carter asked. "What's next in your master plan?"

"I don't have one, but it can't hurt to make contact if we can. I'm thinking that if we get on his good side, we might want to ask him some questions. Informal style. Zach's profile said that the killer wants praise, and he won't hesitate to lie. He'll make up stories to make himself feel like a hero, worthy of a female's admiration."

Carter rolled his eyes and groaned. "You mean this is all because he didn't get enough love from his mother? Shit."

"Zach does think that a significant female in the killer's life triggered this behavior but we don't know why."

Mallory took a deep breath, calming her jangled nerves. She would be inches from a serial killer. She'd agreed to it because it was the right thing to do and she wasn't going to show any fear. Carter would pounce on that like a lion on chateaubriand.

"And I look like her."

Jason gave her a sympathetic look. "That's our theory. Nothing is going to happen to you, I promise. If he even starts to reach out to lay a hand on you, he'll be pulling back a stump. You're as safe as a kitten."

She believed that. It was the only reason she'd agreed to do this.

✦   ✦   ✦

IT TOOK ANOTHER twenty minutes to work their way through the line. The entire time Mallory kept one eye on Peter without being obvious about it. He looked completely harmless, chatting to the other guests whom he seemed to know well. Even physically he didn't appear that intimidating, which was probably to his advantage. He wouldn't strike fear into a female's heart just standing next to her. He seemed…almost meek. If not meek, maybe…affable? Not like a man with a major anger management problem. If Jason hadn't uncovered the evidence he had, she wasn't sure she would have believed that this guy could be their killer.

Stationing herself next to the wreath with all the red roses, Mallory leaned closer to softly run her finger on the edge of a velvety petal. She didn't have to move to smell their heady perfume, however. The aroma of flowers hung heavy in the air, the mixture almost sickly sweet. A shadow fell over her and the bouquet.

"Are they your favorite?"

She turned to see the exact man she'd hoped for. Peter. He'd taken the bait. Okay, Jason said she wasn't bait but it felt like it.

"Actually, I prefer tulips but these are pretty."

He also reached out to caress a bloom. Not close enough to touch her but too close to make her feel comfortable. She tensed and her heart beat against her ribs but she gritted her teeth until her jaw ached, determined not to let him know that he had any effect on her. Sweat pooled at the back of her neck but outward-ly she hoped she looked calm and cool.

"Did you know strawberries are actually part of the rose fam-ily?"

Mallory did but she pretended not to.

"Really? I had no idea. I don't think I'll ever look at a straw-berry the same."

And she wouldn't but not for the reasons he thought. Instead she'd be thinking of this moment. She didn't want red roses either. Ever.

"My name's Peter. Peter Walker. I haven't seen you around here before."

His roundabout way of asking who the hell she was. Of course he knew and he'd seen her, just not here. That's when a thought occurred to her. Matt's parents had expected him to be in attendance. Had he expected her? Had he perhaps even implanted the idea in Don and Gina's minds?

Now she felt sick to her stomach. Ick.

Steadying her voice, she did her best to give him a casual smile. "It's nice to meet you, Peter. I'm Mallory Cook."

Since she didn't want to answer the question of why she was here, she'd just ignore it. Would he be so gauche as to ask it again? She hoped not.

"Mallory," he repeated. "Lovely name for a lovely girl."

Did he actually think he was smooth? Some sort of ladies' man?

"Thank you." The words were forced out through her tight throat, the constriction making breathing and speaking difficult. She was supposed to be getting him to talk but her revulsion was simply too strong. She didn't want to chat with him. She wanted to turn around and flee as quickly as possible. Her fingers tightened on the red cup in her hand and she contemplated raising it. Carter and Jason were hovering not far away, in her peripheral vision, and they would intervene. This would be over and she wouldn't have to stand next to Peter anymore, smelling these roses and his cheap cologne. He looked so confident as if the outcome of this meeting was already decided.

As if he thought he was in complete control of the situation. *Of her.*

She took a step back when Peter reached out with both hands, breaking off a bud from the stem. Wordlessly he lifted it so it was in front of her face before holding it out in offering. Frozen in place, she couldn't make her arm move to accept it. Her throat closed up as she stared into his lifeless dark eyes, glassy and dull. He reminded her of those sharks she'd seen on the nature channel, driven by instinct and hunger. No empathy, no emotion. Even the air surrounding him felt colder as if a cloud followed him around, obliterating the warmth of the sun. Adrenaline flooded her veins and she the hairs on the back of her neck stand up, a red flag she depended on to tell her when she was in danger. The voices in her head were all screaming loudly, drowning out the noise in the room. It was like a freight train roaring against her eardrums.

Run.

"A woman as beautiful as you are should have lots of roses, Mallory. Go ahead. Take it. No one will mind. There are plenty here."

This time she did extend her hand but not for the flower. She raised her hand with the cup in it, holding it out to her right. She wanted far away from him.

Chapter Thirty-Six

THE MINUTE CARTER saw Mallory raise her cup with her right hand he was in motion, Jason on his heels. He didn't know what had spooked her and he didn't care. All he wanted to do was make sure she was okay. Clearly her conversation with Peter had disturbed her. Her face had gone pale and her lips were pressed together in a thin line of distaste.

Peter, on the other hand, didn't appear to recognize that the woman he was speaking to was disturbed. He was wearing a smile that he probably thought was charming but came off cocky and arrogant.

Carter's arm slid around Mallory's waist, hopefully reassuring her that he was there and he would be whenever she needed him. "Hey hon, are you ready to go?"

She looked up at him and nodded, gratitude in her expression. "I think I am. How about you?"

Jason had also joined them but his attention was on Peter. "We could go get some coffee. I saw a diner not far away."

Not sure what his cousin had in mind, Carter readily agreed as did Mallory. Jason held out his hand to Peter.

"I'm Jason Anderson, and I'm one of the members of the

task force working on Matt Montgomery's murder. You were a friend of his, correct?"

Peter smiled widely as if Matt wasn't six feet under currently, shaking Jason's hand. "His best friend since childhood. I'm Peter Walker."

"I don't suppose I could buy you a cup of coffee, Peter? I'd love to talk to you about Matt. Ask you about his life and habits. You know, all the little details are what breaks a case like this. You could be the hero that leads us up the right path. I'll bet you knew Matt better than anybody."

Jason knew what he was doing. Peter preened under the praise, obviously enjoying the idea of being a hero, just as Zach's profile said he would. Jason had also used the word *you* several times, making the conversation all about Peter.

And he clearly liked that, too.

Peter glanced around the room and then shrugged. "Sure, I can do that. I've got the day off and I wouldn't mind some coffee. But you don't want to go to that diner down the road. Follow me and I'll take you to a great little place that serves the best coffee for hundreds of miles."

More boasting and arrogance. Carter already didn't like the little shit, murder or not.

"Sounds great," Jason said. "We'll be happy to follow you."

And Wyatt and Zach too, but Peter didn't need to know that.

Peter gave Mallory a blinding smile. So much for grieving for a friend.

"You can ride with me if you like."

Oh fuck no. Not in this lifetime.

Carter tightened his hold around her waist but kept his voice friendly, although he wanted to kick this smarmy jerk's ass. "She's with me."

Peter never took his eyes from Mallory, as if Carter didn't exist. "The offer's open, Mallory."

"I think I'll ride with Carter, but thank you," she murmured, moving closer to Carter. "Is it far to where we're going?"

Good question. For all they knew Peter was trying to take them out in the middle of nowhere or he was planning to drive off to get away from them.

"Just a few miles off the main drag. Corner of Euclid and Elm. Cute little coffeehouse called The Copper Cup. You'll love it. They have the best pastry in the world. The owner is a good friend of mine."

More boasting. This was getting old fast.

Within fifteen minutes they were all sitting around a circular table near the front window of the little coffeehouse. Peter hadn't tried to make a run for it but Carter almost wished he had. The way the man was looking at Mallory, barely able to drag his attention away was almost obscene. He wasn't bothering to hide his interest. No, his *obsession.* If they hadn't known Peter was the stalker he'd certainly be a suspect after this disgusting display.

"So, Peter," Jason said loudly to bring the man's attention back to them and away from Mallory. "We're anxious to hear what you can tell us about Matt. We need to find whomever did this to him and you might be able to help us."

Finally, Peter stopped staring at Mallory, thanking the waitress when she brought their coffees.

"I've known Matt since we were kids in grade school so you could definitely say I knew him better than anyone else. I was his best friend and vice versa. We spent almost every minute hanging out with each other every summer in high school when I came to visit my dad."

"You moved away?" Jason asked, his hands wrapped around the coffee cup. They'd discussed strategy in the car on the way over and they'd decided to leave the questioning to the professional. Carter and Mallory would take a back seat, staying quiet unless Jason or Peter addressed them directly.

"My mom and dad divorced when I was in seventh grade, and I moved with Mom to Billings and we lived with my grandparents. So I spent the summers here with my dad. Eventually after I graduated from high school I moved back."

Interesting. Most teenagers would have been given a choice as to where to live. Had Peter? It sounded like he'd wanted to live with his dad since he'd moved back right away. Had his mother been abusive? Was that why women were his victims? More questions, but no answers. Did it even matter? It didn't answer the biggest questions they had.

"What do you do for a living?"

"I manage my dad's hardware store." Peter laughed. "Hey, wait a minute. I thought you wanted to ask about Matt, not me."

"That's true," Jason conceded. "What can you tell us about Matt? His interests, his other friends, his job. Was he troubled lately? Upset or angry? Did he have any arguments with anyone in the last few weeks before he died?"

Peter leaned forward, his elbows on the scarred oak table.

"Listen, I don't like to speak ill of the dead and of Matt especially."

But you're going to anyway…

"But I think you need to know that Matt was into something
before he died."

*Bingo. This guy is going to throw his friend under the bus in
3…2…1…*

"What was he into?"

"I'm not sure. All I know is that he was very secretive about
it. He stopped inviting me over to his place. We always had to
hang out at my house or at the bar he was working at. Whenever
I asked him about it, he wouldn't answer and he'd quickly
change the subject. He became more erratic, often being late
when we'd set a time to meet."

"Do you think it was something illegal?"

"Yeah. Yeah, I think he was. He would get tense whenever
we'd see a cop and he wouldn't tell me how he was spending his
time. He definitely had secrets with those people at the bar.
Have you talked to them yet?"

"I have." Jason didn't elaborate. "What else can you tell me
about Matt? Did he have a girlfriend?"

Seemingly not bothered by the question, Peter took a sip of
his coffee. "He dated a lot of girls but I wouldn't say he had
much luck with the ladies. Matt had a temper and I didn't like
him being around any of the girls I dated."

"Because you thought he might hurt them?"

Whatever loyalty Peter might have had to Matt when he was
alive was certainly gone now.

"I saw him slap some girl once that he was dating. Like I

said, he had a temper. When he was angry enough there was no telling what he might do. He was unpredictable."

Carter couldn't keep quiet. "Do you think he could have stabbed one of his girlfriends?"

Luckily Jason didn't seem upset about Carter butting in to the questioning, staying silent so that Peter had to answer.

"If he was mad enough…sure." Peter looked around the cafe and then leaned in, his voice low. "I thought about that when I heard about those girls getting stabbed."

This time it was Mallory who spoke. "Why did you think of Matt?"

"He had a knife and he knew how to use it," Peter replied as if the answer was obvious. "Plus, I met one of those girls. She was with Matt and then she turned up dead."

"Which one?" Jason asked, getting the conversation back on track. "Did you know her name?"

"I met her but I don't remember her name. Jessica? Jane, maybe? I'm not sure. It was the one that they found in the park behind Mallory's house."

Bam. We've got him. He doesn't know what he just revealed.

Peter was still acting like nothing was wrong. He didn't have a clue what he'd let slip inadvertently. Zach's profile had been correct. The killer would want to dazzle them with all the things that he knew. He wanted to impress them. Scratch that. He wanted to impress Mallory.

Mallory looked shaken but to Jason's credit he wasn't fazed in the least. Carter wanted to jump out of his chair and yell but he had to force himself to keep his expression bland. He wasn't made for this cop work. It was all he could do not to slam his fist into Peter Walker's pale, insipid face. This guy was garbage. He didn't give a shit about anyone or anything other than himself. He didn't have friends…he had victims.

Jason shifted in his chair and glanced quickly at Carter before continuing. "I'm going to tell you something that the public doesn't know but I have to ask you to keep it quiet."

This was to draw the little shit in, make him feel important.

It worked. Peter puffed up with importance and nodded solemnly. "I can keep a secret."

That might be the first true thing he'd said all morning.

"The police matched the knife wounds on Matt to the knife wounds on those girls. It was the same weapon. Matt couldn't have hurt those young women. It was someone else. We think it was someone Matt knew because otherwise they probably wouldn't get close enough to kill him. He was a pretty big guy."

"Maybe they surprised him."

Carter had a question and he wasn't going to hold back. "If you thought Matt might have killed those girls, why didn't you go to the police?"

For the first time, Peter seemed off balance and defensive. He wasn't in control of this meeting and he didn't like it. "I didn't have any evidence. Just a gut feeling."

"I always follow my gut," Carter said. "It's never led me down the wrong path."

Peter's lip curled. "I would imagine being an Anderson helps with that."

It was a good thing Carter had had his last name thrown in his face for pretty much his whole life. Otherwise he might have shoved his boot up this guy's ass. Jason, however, must have not had as much confidence in Carter's response because he immediately cut in with another question.

"Would you be willing to let us look at your phone and computer for emails and texts from Matt? It might help us find out who killed him."

Peter was already shaking his head before Jason finished the sentence. "I don't think I can do that. That would be helping the cops to pin a murder on a dead man that can't defend himself. That doesn't seem right. He was my friend and I want him to be able to rest in peace."

So *now* Peter was going to be loyal? A little late in the game.

"What about those other girls?" This was from Mallory and she looked pissed. He reached under the table for her hand and gave it a squeeze but it didn't change the red flags of color on her cheeks. After all the pressure she'd been under this week, he couldn't blame her for reaching the end of her rope. She appeared to be officially done. "Don't they deserve to rest in peace? Or do they even matter?"

Peter didn't answer, instead draining his coffee cup before levering to his feet. He wasn't happy and he was shooting nasty looks at Mallory. Apparently he didn't like women to say too much. Or have opinions.

Tough luck, asshole.

"I think I have someplace to be."

Back to his lair to figure out how to get to Mallory and shut her up for good? Never going to happen as long as Carter breathed oxygen.

Jason held up one finger as he tapped at his phone. "Just a second, Peter. You might be interested in this case development."

"I'm not interested in you railroading my friend and making him a murderer."

Jason finally looked up and then handed his phone to Carter. A cursory reading of the text displayed had Carter grinning.

"We're not interested in turning your friend into a murderer. He did that himself," Jason said. "With a little help from you."

Carter held up Jason's phone. "Funny thing about emails and texts, Peter. They go both ways. We already have them from Matt's phone and laptop. He tried to delete them but nothing ever really goes away. It took our guys some time but they managed to resurrect your messages to each other. All of them. Looks like you two were working together. The police are on their way."

Carter should have expected it after what he'd just said but it was still a surprise. Peter's eyes grew wide as he realized what he was hearing. Moving quickly, he shoved his chair back so that it fell and skidded along the floor and then bolted for the door, the bell above ringing cheerily despite the situation.

Jason glared at Carter. "Fuck, why did you tell him that the police are on their way? Now he's on the run. I take back what I said. You'd make a lousy cop."

Shrugging, Carter threw up his hands. "Sorry, I was on a roll. Now what do we do?"

Jason pointed to himself and Mallory and then Carter. "Not we. You. You made him run so you get to catch him. You're always bragging about what great shape you're in."

Shit. Carter hadn't done any training since all of this bullshit started at the rest stop.

Pushing his own chair back, Carter cursed his choice of footwear today. Instead of his comfy and supportive running shoes, he was wearing his dress boots. They were not made for running but he had little choice. He hit the door at a jog, looking right and left for the little worm. He wasn't difficult to find. He'd crossed the street and was running south down Euclid Avenue. Clearly he was out of shape because Carter could see him huffing and puffing from here, frantically looking over his shoulder. The air was sharp and cold, and sucking that into his lungs was going to hurt like a bitch if he wasn't used to it.

Carter – with the exception of the last week – did this almost every day of his life. After training for that obstacle course with his brothers, he'd found that he actually enjoyed running.

He put on a burst of speed to catch up to Peter who was do-ing his damnedest to stay ahead. There was only about ten feet between them and Carter could hear the other man's labored breathing even from that distance. He wouldn't last much longer but Carter could do this all day if he had to. He would chase him to the ends of the earth to remove him as a threat from Mallory's life.

His prediction turned out to be true. A half a block later, Carter caught up with Peter, grabbing the back of his jacket and throwing him to the ground. Peter clutched his side and went down on the sidewalk, sucking wind and whining about how unfair it all was, too tired to put up much of a fight. Carter immediately went down on top of him, his knee in the squirm-ing man's lower back and pinning him to the ground. Sirens wailed in the background. The cops were almost there and they would take Peter away. With any luck, he'd never see the light of day again or threaten another woman.

Carter couldn't stop himself from leaning down to whisper in Peter's ear.

"You'll never get near her. Do you understand me? Never. Not while I'm around."

Peter growled something Carter couldn't make out and then tried to buck him off but he didn't succeed. They stayed in that same position until a swarm of cops came and pulled Carter off of Peter, cuffing the other man behind his back and leading him away. Jason and Mallory must have made their way from the coffee shop because she threw herself at him, her arms tight around his waist. He buried his face in her fragrant hair and breathed deeply. This woman had become everything in such a short time. How did it happen? Who cared? It had and he wasn't sorry. This was what his brothers and cousins talked about.

I understand now. I'd die for her.

Jason slapped him on the back while Mallory clung to him, tears rolling down her cheeks. Happiness? Relief? A mixture of all of it, probably. He held her just as tightly, not wanting to break the contact. She felt so good in his arms.

"You did good. You got him," Jason said.

"We got him," Carter corrected. "I couldn't have done this alone. I'm no cop, remember?"

"You didn't do too bad," Jason chuckled. "When you were needed you were there. That's the important thing. Wyatt is going to drive you and Mallory back home. I'm going with the cops to interrogate our suspect. Your part is ending but our part is just beginning. We have a lot of work to do to put him behind bars for good but I think we're building a solid case. You can relax now, Mallory. You're safe."

She wiped at her cheeks and smiled. So beautiful. "Thank you, Jason. And to Wyatt and Zach and all the other men that helped. I really appreciate it."

Carter leaned back so he could look into her face. "Hey, what am I? Chopped liver?"

She tugged at the collar of his shirt so he had to bend over close to her perfect pink lips.

"I have a special thank you for when we get home," she whispered, for his ears only.

Hot damn. This love stuff was working out just fine.

Chapter Thirty-Seven

A S QUIETLY AS possible, Mallory slipped on her shoes and smoothed down her hair. It had to be a rat's nest by now. She and Carter had spent the last several hours doing debauched things to one another in his king-sized bed and now he was snoring, exhausted from their activities. All she wanted to do was curl up next to him and sleep as well but that was her body and heart talking. Her mind? That was a different story.

Her stalker was in jail. She wasn't in danger anymore. That was a good thing. But she couldn't help but think back over the last week. Her relationship with Carter had been fueled by fear, danger, and about a thousand other heightened emotions. He'd gone into protector mode practically from that first moment at the rest stop. But he didn't need to do that now. Would it change things? Would he be different?

Old enough to know her own mind, Mallory wasn't questioning her own feelings. She had fallen in love with Carter Anderson whether for good or bad.

Carter, too, was a grown man. Older than her, he ought to know his own mind as well. But…clearly he'd never been in any kind of serious relationship. He'd admitted to partying and womanizing, never taking dating to the next level. She had to admit that it was hard to trust that his feelings were genuine and not a product of all that had happened in the last week.

A week. Was that all it had been? Nine days since their first date and life would never be the same. It was a short time to fall in love. She'd been cautious most of her life and she wanted to believe…

The last time she had though, she'd been burned.

Putting her purse over her shoulder, she turned to look at Carter one last time. The air was heavy with sleep and his features were relaxed and serene. He was so handsome, almost beautiful, which was a funny word to describe a man but it fit this circumstance. At this angle, with his muscled torso on display, he looked like he'd been chiseled from marble.

If he'd only been good looking she would have been fine, but he had to be smart, charming, and protective, too. If he didn't feel the same, getting over him wasn't going to be easy. Finding another man like him would probably prove impossible.

For a moment she hesitated in the bedroom doorway. If she stayed, not giving him a chance to think things over, it might all turn out okay. They could be happy and in love. All hunky and dory. Except that didn't seem fair. He deserved a chance to breathe and decide what he really wanted. She could give him that and she would.

If he wanted her that was great. If he didn't, then it wasn't meant to be. She couldn't force him to feel the same. The thought pierced at her vulnerable heart, though. She was afraid that stepping back might give him a chance to remember all the fun he had as a wild single man. She couldn't compete with dozens of younger, more beautiful women.

You have to do this. Give him the space he's lacked this last week.

With more resolve than she ever thought she had, Mallory walked out of the bedroom and softly closed the door. No going back now.

Would he decide that he wanted her or would he happily return to his carefree womanizing ways?

She'd have to wait to find out.

CARTER DIDN'T KNOW whether to be mad or proud of Mallory. When he'd woken up last night, all alone in a cold empty bed and found that stupid, rambling note, he'd been angry and frantic to find her. He couldn't argue that they'd gotten together under strange circumstances. That was a given.

But dammit, he didn't need any *time* or *space* to figure out how he felt. He'd fallen in love with her and he was happy about it. He wanted to be with her and she was putting unnecessary distance between them.

He couldn't, however, deny the fact that he was proud of her for having the courage to walk away. To give him that space and time that she thought he might need. He wasn't so sure if the shoe was on the other foot that he'd have the strength to do the same. She thought he might want to return to his old life but even before meeting her he'd already decided that he was done with that.

So of course he'd pulled on his pants and ran after her, driving like a bat out of hell to her home. He'd been even more pissed off when he got there to find that she was nowhere to be found. He'd pounded on her front door but there hadn't been any movement or sound inside. The neighbors had given him some serious side eye, however. A couple walking their dog had glared so hard at him he was sure they were going to have the police come and take him away. Once he'd returned home and calmed down he realized that he knew exactly where she'd be the next morning.

School.

Mallory would be returning to work so all he had to do was be there to meet her. She wouldn't be able to avoid him. That's how he found himself standing at the entrance to her school right by the teacher's parking lot. He was holding a bouquet of flowers and so far he'd attracted quite a bit of attention, mostly smiles and indulgent giggles. One woman had stopped in front of him, her gaze raking him head to toe.

"Hey there, handsome. Are those flowers for me?"

He'd given her a regretful smile. "Sorry, they're for my girl-friend."

She'd given in gracefully, shrugging as she opened the door. "Lucky girl. If she doesn't want them, give me a call."

In the twenty minutes he'd been standing here waiting quite a crowd had gathered, pressing their noses against the glass windows and doors. Everyone seemed to waiting for him to either have a romantic reunion or to get his ass kicked.

When Mallory finally drove into the parking lot, his heart lurched in his chest and he was suddenly far more nervous than he'd expected to be. With every passing moment doubt had begun to build in his gut and he could taste the acid in the back of his throat.

What if she only said what she did because she wanted to let him down easy? What if she didn't feel the same and he was about to get his heart broken? Why would an amazing woman like Mallory want to be with a guy like him? He had a pretty terrible past, after all. Not all women would be able to overlook it and just focus on the future. Maybe she'd stayed with him because he was protecting her but now that she'd come to know him a bit better she couldn't stand him.

Then he thought about how they made love, the way she touched him and the sighs and moans that came out of her mouth. He simply couldn't believe that she could be like that with him and not feel…something.

His chest tightened as Mallory walked toward him, her expression first surprised, then questioning, and finally happy. Her smile was genuine and so was the love he saw in her eyes as she stopped in front of him. Blood roared in his ears as he held out the flowers.

"Hi."

Carter had a whole speech planned but he couldn't remember a word of it, reduced instead to a one syllable greeting.

"Hi."

She'd never looked more beautiful than this moment. Her long hair was shiny and pulled back in a ponytail that showed off her lovely face. She was wearing a conservative black skirt and white blouse but he didn't need fancy lingerie to get his motor going. She was a knockout. All she needed was a pair of glasses perched on her nose and she could be the sexy librarian of his dreams.

"You shouldn't have left. I didn't need any time to think about it."

"It's a big decision. I didn't want you to feel pressured. Our situation was…"

Her voice trailed off but he could fill in the blank.

"It was," he agreed, closing the gap between them so he could smell her shampoo and feel the heat from her body. "But it doesn't change what I feel."

She had to lean back a little to look in his eyes. "What do you feel, Carter?"

It was time to man up. Say the words. Funny, he'd thought it would be so difficult but when the right woman was standing in front of him it was so easy.

"I love you, Mallory. I know it's fast and I know we have a long way to go but I love you."

She blinked a few times and a tear slid down her creamy cheek. "I love you, too."

A cheer went up from the crowd that had gathered, startling them both. There were at least twice the number of people than the last time he'd looked and most of those that had been inside the building were now outside of it, clapping and exhorting them to kiss.

He didn't have any objections to that. It sounded like a great idea.

"They want us to kiss."

She raised an eyebrow, her gaze running over her fellow teachers. "I'll never hear the end of it if we don't and I'll never hear the end of it if we do."

His hand cupped her cheek. "So we might as well do as we

please."

Their lips touched and the rest of the world faded away. They had an audience but Carter didn't care. They might as well have not existed for all the notice he took. His world narrowed to this one incredible woman. Thank heaven he'd gone on that blind date.

He raised his head and smiled, thinking about all they had to look forward to. So many firsts as a couple. "Come to Sunday dinner, Mallory? As my official girlfriend?"

"I'd love to."

It was only the beginning for them.

Chapter Thirty-Eight

One year and a few months later…

CARTER'S MOTHER KATHY held up the open magazine for Mallory's inspection. "What do you think? The tables are gorgeous. We could do something like that but with the flowers you prefer."

Mallory leaned forward and squinted her eyes. Her glasses were in her purse and she'd left it in the living room. The flower arrangements were all roses and everyone in the Anderson family knew how she felt about roses, but Kathy had a good eye for details. She was right about how lovely the rest of the table design was.

"I like it," she pronounced. "But Carter has to look at it, too. He wants to be part of every decision."

Sunday dinner had been eaten and the dining table cleared so that the women could look through bridal magazines to their hearts' content and start making plans for Mallory and Carter's wedding in the summer. He'd asked on Christmas Eve and now they had less than six months to put it all together.

The venue was easy. They both wanted to be married on the

ranch. They'd rent a huge tent and invite everyone they'd ever met. Mallory had been leaning toward a small ceremony but it appeared that when Carter Anderson got married it was the event of the century. People from all over the globe were planning on attending their late June nuptials.

Brinley rolled her eyes. "Every decision? Jason only cared about the flavor of the cake. Everything else he left to me."

"I'm only going to do this once." Carter had quietly joined them to sneak a bite of her apple pie. He didn't even pretend, not bothering to give her back the fork. "This *wedding is for the bride, honeymoon is for the groom* is so twentieth century. I want a wedding that reflects both of us."

Jason slapped Carter on the back before leaning down to kiss Brinley on the cheek. "Then you're going to have a craft beer bar, I assume? And twenty kinds of cheesecake?"

Mallory didn't mind the craft beer but twenty kinds of cheesecake was a little over the top. But this man she was marrying…he was over the top. It was a trait she loved about him. Everything he did was all out. No half measures.

"Maybe," Carter replied cheekily, settling into the chair next to Mallory. "Where in the hell have you been, anyway? You missed dinner."

"Some of us have to work on a Sunday."

Brinley stood and pushed her husband into a chair. "I'll go fill you a plate. Relax a little."

Jason sat heavily into the chair. "I could sleep for a week and I just might do it. We finally finished a pain in the ass case. All of us were working on it."

"Then you should celebrate," Kathy said, patting his hand.

"Take some time off."

Jason nodded in agreement. "I might do that. We've been talking about taking the kids to Disney World. The weather would be nice in Florida." His smile fell and his expression grew serious. "I also got a call today. There's news about Walker. If you want it."

Carter's fingers tightened on her thigh but he stayed silent. He would want to know whatever it was that Jason knew but did she? She'd moved on and it had been months since she'd heard that name. Walker's lawyer had filed several pre-trial motions that had made the news but mostly the justice system ground away slowly and silently.

"I do," she finally said. She couldn't deny her interest in the case. There were days she wondered if he would ever go to trial. So far, he was held at the county jail but if he was found guilty he'd go to the state prison. If he was found innocent...

She couldn't really comprehend that outcome. As far as she was concerned, the evidence that Jason's team had gathered, and more had been obtained since his arrest, the case was overwhelming against him.

"Walker has decided to plead guilty," Jason said. "His lawyer is getting the papers ready to file right now."

"And in return?" Carter growled, his body tense next to hers. "What does Walker get?"

"Death penalty is off the table. Life with no possibility of parole. All he has to do is admit to his crimes in detail."

Peter Walker had already given several interviews to reporters, naming Matt Montgomery as his accomplice in the murders of the first two women. He and Matt would see a woman at the bar, stalk her, and then kill her. Except that Matt had "fallen" for the third woman. Peter and Matt had argued at the bar that night and Matt had taken off to warn the young woman. Peter had snuck into Matt's trunk, expecting to hop out at the female's home – where he would kill them both – only to be surprised that Matt had stopped at the rest area. Having no choice now that Matt knew what he'd done, he'd had to kill his friend then and there before running off into the woods and to the bar off of the highway where he'd stolen a car to get home. He'd dumped the vehicle about a mile from his house and no one had connected the car theft with the murder. Later he'd killed the girl but he'd already chosen his next victim from the news report about the murder.

Mallory.

"As long as he's behind bars for the rest of his life," she said. "That's the important thing. No one else is going to get hurt. I think I'm going to get another piece of pie. Anyone want another?"

"I want one," Carter declared, trailing after her into the kitchen where Brinley was just finishing warming Jason's dinner. She gave them a smile and bustled out to the dining room carrying a full plate, leaving them alone. "Are you okay, babe?"

"I'm fine. I think that might be the last time we have to hear his name." Mallory cut another slice of pie and handed it to Carter. "For you, gorgeous. Stop eating mine."

He dug right in, his appetite enormous. "But I thought we were supposed to share everything."

"I won't share my dessert. Next time you'll get a fork in the knuckles. You've been warned."

Not that it would matter. She'd warned him before.

"You're one tough lady. I like that about you."

She tilted her head and waggled her brows like he was known to do.

"Oh yeah? What else do you like about me?"

"Every single solitary thing," he responded immediately. "You know, I worship you so much I should probably marry you. What do you think about that idea?"

He was in a goofy mood.

"I think that you already asked me and I said yes."

He leaned down and pressed a quick kiss to her lips. He tasted like sugar and cinnamon.

"I don't know what I would have done if you'd said no."

"Asked again. Wore me down until I gave in. You're annoying like that."

"But you love me that way."

She did and she would. Forever and always. Kathy had once said that when a woman or a man falls for an Anderson, it stuck for life.

Stuck together. It sounded over the top. And just right.

I hope you enjoyed Carter and Mallory's happily ever after! Thank you for reading Road to Danger!

Don't miss a thing! Sign up to be notified of Olivia's new releases:

oliviajaymesoptin.instapage.com

About The Author

Olivia Jaymes is a wife, mother, lover of sexy romance, and caffeine addict. She lives with her husband, son, and two spoiled dogs in central Florida, spending her days with handsome alpha males and spunky heroines.

She is currently working on a new contemporary romance series to debut in the fall of 2018. She also writes The Hollywood Showmance Chronicles in addition to the ongoing Danger Incorporated series and the Cowboy Justice Association series.

Visit Olivia Jaymes at

www.OliviaJaymes.com

Other Titles by Olivia Jaymes

Danger Incorporated
Damsel In Danger
Hiding From Danger
Discarded Heart Novella
Indecent Danger
Embracing Danger
Danger In The Night
Reunited With Danger
Window to Danger

Cowboy Justice Association
Cowboy Command
Justice Healed
Cowboy Truth
Cowboy Famous
Cowboy Cool
Imperfect Justice
The Deputies
Justice Inked
Justice Reborn
Vengeful Justice

Military Moguls

Champagne and Bullets

Diamonds and Revolvers

Caviar and Covert Ops

Emeralds, Rubies, and Camouflage

Midnight Blue Beach

Wicked After Midnight

Midnight Of No Return

Kiss Midnight Goodbye

The Hollywood Showmance Chronicles

A Kiss For the Cameras

Swinging From A Star

Wild on the Red Carpet

Love in the Spotlight